A SEASON FOR HOPE

Fairhope, Book 3

SARRA CANNON

Dead River Books

Cover Designed by Najla Qamber Designs.

Editing services by Janet Bessey at Dragonfly Editing.

Want to be notified of new releases and exciting giveaways from Sarra
Cannon? Join the Mailing List now.

🕸 Created with Vellum

To Kylene Noel
You're not just my cousin,
you're also one of my best friends.
Seeing you at Christmas was a
highlight of growing up.
Thankful for you this season
and always.

PROLOGUE

I glance up at the clock on the wall.

It's two minutes after and the professor is still talking. If he doesn't wrap it up soon, I'm going to stab myself in the eye with this pencil.

Under the table, my toes tap against the ugly green carpet. My bookbag is already packed up. I sling it across my shoulder and sit at the edge of my chair. The girl next to me gives me the stink-eye and I'm tempted to stick my tongue out at her, but instead, I just look at the clock again.

Preston is waiting for me. Yesterday, he texted and said he had something really important he wanted to talk to me about, and I haven't been able to calm the butterflies in my stomach since.

We've been together for just over three years, but the past few months have been rocky to say the least.

I'm praying he wants to talk about how we can reconnect. I've been bugging him about us taking a trip together over the holidays, but he doesn't want to leave his twin sister,

Penny, since she's newly pregnant and had some complications in the early months. I completely understand that, but at the same time, I'm desperate to bring his attention back to me.

Most of our relationship has been a never-ending push and pull. I pull him toward me, he pushes away. I push him to make more of a commitment and he pulls farther away. I've learned to be a good-time girl, always going with the flow and being careful not to demand too much of him.

But the things that used to work with him aren't working anymore.

I swallow, my mouth dry as a bone.

I have a bottle of water in my bag, but I'm not about to open it back up. My fingers tremble and I squeeze my pencil tighter, taking down the last few notes as the professor finally wraps up the lesson.

This is our last class before the Thanksgiving break, so I guess he wanted to make the most of it, but I'm so done. I've barely been listening as it is today. My notes make zero sense, but I don't even care. I just want to bolt.

The moment he dismisses us, I push through the throng of students and make a run for the exit. I'm out of breath by the time I push out into the cold afternoon air. I breathe in and out, my heart racing. My stomach feels sick with worry. Whenever your long-time boyfriend says he needs to talk it can only mean one of two things. Either he's wanting more. Or he's breaking up with you.

I shiver and pull my coat tight, wrapping my scarf around my neck and over my lips.

He asked me to meet him at his car, so I'm hoping he's planning to take me to dinner. I dressed up more than normal just in case but these high-heeled boots aren't the best for jogging across campus. I force myself to slow down, mentally kicking myself for being so nervous. So desperate.

Preston has his own parking spot on campus. It's one of the perks of being a Wright. He's practically royalty in this town because he comes from the wealthiest family in the state of Georgia. His great-grandfather started Fairhope Coastal University and his parents are still huge contributors.

As I turn the corner of the administration building, his sleek black BMW comes into view and my heart catapults into my throat. He's sitting on the hood fiddling with his cell phone. I smile as he turns toward the sound of my boots clacking against the sidewalk.

But the way he smiles back—all sad and sorry—is like a punch straight in my gut.

He doesn't want to reconnect with me.

My legs grow weak and I struggle to keep it together. I've worn a mask for him a hundred times before, and I'm good at it. The happy, carefree girlfriend. Always up for a good time. The girl who never asks for more than what I have right this moment.

Once I realized those kinds of demands only put distance between us, I learned how to be what he wanted me to be. Easy and fun.

But today I'm struggling to keep the mask in place.

"Hi," I say. I set my backpack down on the sidewalk and lean into him. When I go to kiss him, he turns his head at the last second and my lips settle on his cheek.

I almost dissolve into frantic tears and it takes an enormous amount of self-control not to.

Deep inside, my brain is refusing to believe what my

heart already knows. This can't really be happening. Not after everything we've been through. Not now, please.

"Hey," he says. He stands and slips his phone into his back pocket. He doesn't touch me and the absence of affection might as well be a slap across my face. "Can we go somewhere?"

I want to say no. Part of me wants to tell him that I'd rather he just got it over with so I can get home and move on with my life. But part of me knows that right now, I have no life outside of Preston Wright.

"Sure," I say. "Do you want to go to dinner or something?"

He draws his bottom lip into his mouth. "I was thinking maybe we could just go back to your place," he says. "Maybe take a walk on the boardwalk for a few?"

My apartment is on the other side of campus, really close to the beach and the long wooden boardwalk that leads up to the pier.

"Great, yeah," I say, playing my part of the agreeable girlfriend.

Always.

The ride to the boardwalk is tense and awkward. I try to start several conversations, but Preston's answers are short and don't leave much room for follow-up. I press my legs together tightly, wanting to curl up into a little ball and hide my face until this whole thing is over.

The tiniest hope still lives in my pit, saying this isn't what I think it is. But ten minutes later, he's walking beside me saying the words I never wanted to hear.

"Life has gotten really complicated lately," he says. "With Penny having a baby and my internship with the company, I haven't had a lot of time to spend with you and I'm really sorry."

"It's okay," I say. I reach for his hand and he squeezes it and lets it go. My heart sinks further into my stomach.

"It's really not," he says. He stops in front of a bench and stares out at the ocean. "I don't know how else to really say this."

I swallow and my mouth feels like it's filled with sand. I can't say anything. I can't even fight for this. All I can do is watch as it slips away.

"I think it's time we both moved on, Bailey." He looks into my eyes and I know there's nothing I can do to change his mind. "The past three years have been amazing, but I feel like I'm changing. I want different things than I wanted a few years ago."

Tears well up in my eyes. "What did I do wrong?" I whisper.

He shakes his head. "You didn't do anything wrong," he says. He smiles. "You're perfect, Bailey. I really care about you. I don't want you to blame yourself. It's just that the past few months have completely changed me. I need some space and some time to figure out where I go from here."

I look down toward my boots, hot tears streaming down my face. I try to tell him what I'm feeling. I want to say that I'll change with him. That I'll figure out a way to be everything he wants. Only, the words won't come. When I open my mouth to speak, a sob chokes me. I lift my hand to my throat and turn away, not wanting him to see me like this.

He clutches my arms and pulls me back toward his warm body. "I'm so sorry," he whispers into my hair. "I never meant to hurt you."

Hurt doesn't even begin to describe what I'm feeling.

Devastated. Smashed. Completely destroyed.

Preston Wright was everything I ever wanted. And as he wraps his arms around my shaking body one last time, the world around me spins faster and faster. I fall down, deep into the blackest of holes. A hopeless place where broken hearts live and die and dreams of the future become memories of something that will never, ever be real.

CHAPTER 1

THREE WEEKS LATER

"Rise and shine."

I open my eyes to slits and groan as my roommate Monica bursts through the door to my room, a tray of juice and eggs in her hands. She pulls the shades up and sunlight streams into the room.

I sink deeper into the comforter, pulling my pillow over my head to block out the light.

Monica yanks the covers off my body and sits down beside me. "You can't lay in this bed for the rest of your life," she says. "Today is the first day of the rest of your life. Now get your gorgeous ass out of bed."

She smacks my thigh and it makes a sharp popping sound. I sit up and rub the area, a red hand print burned onto my skin.

"What the fuck was that for?" I say. I scramble toward the edge of the bed and pull my sheets and comforter off the floor and back up onto the bed. It's cold in here and I had been nice and warm before she barged in like some militant nurse in a nut house.

She picks up the glass of orange juice and holds it out to me. "It was supposed to be motivational," she says. "Now drink your juice like a good girl."

I pout and turn away, trying to recreate my cocoon.

Monica sighs and lays down behind me. She rests her bony chin on my arm. "Come on, Bailey, you've got to get out of bed," she says. "It's been weeks. I'm starting to lose my patience, here."

Anger and guilt go to war inside my chest and familiar tears spring to my eyes. Tears are my best friends lately. I've spent more time with them than anyone else.

"Just leave me alone, then," I say. "I didn't ask you to fix me."

I swipe at the tears but they're falling too fast. They soak into my pillow and my knotted hair. I haven't showered in days.

"When was the last time you ate something?" she asks.

I shrug and close my eyes. "I'm not hungry."

"You have to eat," she says. "You have to get out of this apartment. You're missing too much class, Bailey. I'm worried about you. This week is the last week before finals. If you don't go to class and at least get the notes, you're going to fail."

"I don't care," I say, sniffing. I know I'm being pathetic, but I don't have the energy to be more than this.

"Fine," she says, sitting up. "How about this? You're supposed to work this afternoon. Mr. Edwards said if you called in sick one more time, he was going to have to let you go, didn't he? If you miss work, how are you going to pay rent next month? You're already behind. If I have to, I'll find another roommate and kick you out on your ass."

I turn and sit up. My face is twisted and crumpled. "You'd do that?"

She has her arms crossed in front of her chest and her lips are a thin, tight line. "No," she says, her eyebrows cinched together. "But I will if it means you'll get up and go to work."

My shoulders fall and I reach for a tissue on the nightstand. I blow my nose and wipe my face. "I can't do it," I say. "I'm just so tired all the time."

Monica's voice softens. "You're tired because you sleep all the time," she says. "I promise that if you'd just get up and at least force yourself to go through the motions of being a real human being, you'd start to feel better."

I smile through fresh tears. "I don't feel human."

"I know." She sits beside me and runs her hand through my long hair, pushing a strand behind my ear. "Breaking up sucks balls. I get it. But there's more to life than Preston fucking Wright."

"Is there?" I ask, looking up.

She gives a sad smile and nods. "I guarantee it," she says. "And you're not going to find it laying in here like an invalid."

I pick at the tissue in my hand, pulling it apart until it almost crumbles in my hands. I know she's right, but it's so hard to face everyone. I used to walk onto campus knowing I was the girl everyone envied. I was Preston's girl. I sacrificed a lot to earn that title. And now it's gone. I'm no one anymore.

"It's time," she says. "You did a good 'Bella Swan in the

woods after Edward left' impression, but now it's time to rejoin the land of the living and prove to him he made a huge mistake."

I blow my nose again and swallow back more tears. "Edward came back to Bella, though," I say.

Monica walks to the door, then turns back and shakes her head. "Honey, Preston is not your Edward. Trust me on this."

I laugh as she disappears.

Maybe she's right. Maybe it is time. Although, as I force myself out of bed and into the shower, I wonder at the fairness of only having three weeks to mourn something that took three years to build.

C ampus is packed. A couple of people wave or say hi
as I pass, but I'm already late for work and not
really feeling like being social.

I spent way too much time in the shower, letting the hot
water soak into me, as if it could heal me.

It didn't.

My heart was still broken when I emerged, my skin pink
and raw. I knew I was running late, too, but I couldn't rush
getting ready. I'd already run into Preston once before when
I looked like hell. Red puffy eyes. Knotty hair. No makeup. I
probably looked like I'd been hit by a bus. And the pity in his
eyes was too much to handle.

So I never leave the house anymore without looking
perfect. Or at least not like a homeless person.

The Cup, a coffee shop and cafe where I work, is located
in the student center at the other end of the quad. I decide
to take a short-cut through the Science building because

there's a bridge leading to the student center from there. Plus, it's freezing cold outside.

I'm out of breath as I race up the stairs to the second floor. My feet hit the landing, but before I can reach for the heavy metal door, it flies open. My brain registers the danger, but I'm moving way too fast to stop myself as the door connects with my forehead.

Pain explodes behind my eye and across my cheek. I fall backward. My hands flail, searching for anything that might break my fall. Strong hands reach out and grab my arms.

"Shit, are you okay?" a guy asks.

I can't answer. My vision blurs and the pain spreads like fire across my cheek. I keep my hold on the guy and sink toward the floor, holding both hands up to my eye. Something warm and sticky seeps from a gash above my eye. I pull my trembling hands away and force my eyes open. Bright red blood stares back at me and my stomach churns.

I close my eyes again and take a slow, deep breath in. I'm going to faint.

The guy who hit me throws his bag on the ground and unzips it quickly.

"Lean against the wall," he says, easing me toward the cool cinder-block. He's squatting beside me. "Watch your hands a sec. Let me clean this up so it doesn't get infected."

His voice is calm and soothing, but my heart is thumping and I'm close to tears. I never should have left the apartment. What if the rest of my life is just a series of painful events?

I lower my hands for him, but keep my palms up against my legs, not wanting to wipe the blood on my clean jeans.

He puts his hand under my chin and lifts my face up

toward his. I feel vulnerable and exposed. Stupid. Who gets hit in the face by a door?

For the first time since I was hit, I really open my eyes and look at the guy who hit me. My mouth drops open slightly and I breathe in, a tingle spreading through my veins. He's a few years older than me. A grad student maybe? And he's hot as hell. I study him as he cleans my forehead with an alcohol swab.

His dark-blond hair is long and tousled, dipping down near the collar of his grey t-shirt. As he wipes the blood from my face, the muscles in his arms flex slightly and stretch the material at his bicep. His jeans are worn and his sneakers have holes in them. When he lifts his hand to my head again, I notice a tattoo on the inside of his wrist, but can't see it well enough to make out what it says.

He looks up and sees me studying him. His eyes are hazel with flecks of bright green and something about him suddenly seems so familiar. In my daze I can't quite place him.

He reaches back inside his bag and pulls out a bandage, placing it tenderly over the cut. His fingers linger against my cheek.

I briefly wonder what kind of guy carries alcohol swabs and bandages in his backpack, but the feel of his warm skin against mine distracts me. After being out in the cold wind, I wish I could lean into him.

"Were you a boyscout or something?" I ask, my hand fluttering up toward the bandage. When he looks confused, I add, "The bandages and alcohol."

"Oh," he says, smiling. "Med student."

I raise an eyebrow. "I guess in terms of running into doors, I'm lucky there was a future doctor behind this one."

"That was totally my fault," he says. "I was in a hurry to get to the lab and I came barreling through the door like an asshole. You sure you're okay? Do you feel lightheaded or anything?"

I shake my head and go to stand, but the room spins and I sink back down. "Maybe a little."

"Hang on," he says. "I'll be right back."

He stands and goes back inside to the main second-floor hallway.

I lean my head back against the wall and close my eyes for a second, but everything spins and my stomach lurches. I open my eyes again and take several deep breaths. My hands are trembling.

My life is such a mess right now. I feel like I'm struggling against the tide, a strong undercurrent of sadness constantly dragging me back under. I can't live like this.

The door behind me opens again, and I swipe at the falling tears.

Grey-shirt guy sits down beside me on the stairs. He hands me a plastic cup full of ice water. "This should help some," he says.

"Thanks." I take a sip of the water and hold it in my mouth for a while, letting the cold of it counteract the rolling nausea in my stomach. I swallow and feel the cold liquid make its path down my throat. "Do you need to be somewhere?"

He shakes his head. "No," he says. "I want to stay and make sure you don't need to go to the med center."

"I'm fine, really," I say. I'm not even close to being fine, but he's a stranger and he doesn't need to know that. "You said you were rushing somewhere."

He leans back against the stair rail. "It's not important," he says, his hazel eyes staring straight through me. As if he knows I'm not alright. "Were you heading to a class? I don't think I've seen you in this building before."

"No," I say with a laugh. "I was on my way to work."

"Just my luck," he murmurs.

I turn my head to the side. "What does that mean?"

He shakes his head. "Nothing," he says, the smile taking over his face now.

I can't tear my gaze away from his lips. My stomach flutters and I swallow, feeling slightly breathless.

I want to ask him more, because I feel like there's more to it than that. But I'm crazy late for work and I can't afford to lose my job.

"I should probably get going," I say. I stand slowly and wait for the head rush, but I actually feel okay.

He stands and grabs my bag for me. "You sure you're feeling up to it? I can wait with you here for a while longer if you want," he says.

I shake my head. I have a pounding headache, but I don't think sitting here is going to cure it. "I'm fine. I'm actually pretty late."

"I'll walk with you, then," he says. He opens the door to the second floor and I walk inside. "It's the least I can do after slamming into you like that."

I study him for a second. He's been so sweet and attentive and now he's offering to walk me to work? Talk about a good bedside manner. I thought men like this only existed in fairy tales or made-for-TV movies. There's got to be something wrong with him.

And if there's not, he's way too good for me anyway. Besides, my heart is too broken to even think about being attracted to someone else.

"I'm good," I say. I hand him my empty water glass. "Thanks, though. See you around...?"

"Judd," he says. His fingers brush mine as he takes the glass. "Judd Kohler."

My stomach flutters again, catching me off guard. I turn fast and nearly smack into a water fountain jutting out of the wall. I stumble around it, blushing.

When I get a few steps further, he calls out to me. "Wait."

I stop and look back at him.

"You didn't tell me your name," he says.

"Bailey," I say, unable to control the smile that spreads across my face.

He raises his hand in a wave. "Be careful around doors, Bailey." he says.

"I will." I raise a hand in a half-wave as I disappear down the bridge toward the student center.

It doesn't occur to me until I get all the way to the door of The Cup that I haven't stopped smiling.

CHAPTER 3

Work goes by surprisingly fast. There are a ton of customers today. The semester is winding down and everyone is studying for finals, so I know we'll be busy from here until the Christmas break.

My manager, Mr. Edwards is in good spirits, singing along to the Christmas carols playing on the local radio station. The outside windows have been sprayed with fake snow and we're selling yummy new drinks like peppermint hot chocolate and snickerdoodle lattes.

When I cash out at seven and head back toward my car, there's a spring in my step I thought I'd never get back.

It's dark out and colder than it's been all year. I hitch my backpack higher on my shoulder and shove my hands into the pockets of my purple leather coat.

I hit the sidewalk leading to the main student parking lot and out of habit, glance toward Preston's parking spot. It's late, so I don't expect to see him. But there he is.

The sight of him creates an ache deep inside. I wish there was some kind of tradition where every time you broke up with someone, they had to wear a collar that would beep whenever they got within a hundred yards of you. No more surprise attacks. My heart can't take it.

At first, I only pay attention to him. The curve of his mouth. His dark hair and eyes. His tall, muscular body.

But the sound of laughter pulls me from my self-pity trance and I really open my eyes.

Leaning against the side of his car is a girl with short blond pigtails. I can't see her clearly from here, but I can see him. And the way his eyes shine when he looks at her slices through my soul.

My chest tightens and I breathe in slowly.

Just seeing him is hard enough, but seeing him smiling down at another girl is too much.

I turn and run toward my car, fumbling with the keys. I finally manage to get it started, but by the time I do, my vision is blurred with tears.

I press my head against the headrest and close my eyes. There must be some cosmic rule that says whenever you start to feel happy again after a breakup, the universe must slam you with a surprise sighting just to remind you how much you're hurting.

Will I ever get over this feeling? Will I ever be able to see him and not feel this tight ache in my core?

And the shitty thing is that I knew this was coming. I knew he was pulling away from me. Ever since Leigh Anne, his ex-girlfriend, came back into town this past summer, things were tense between us. Understandably.

Preston may have cheated on Leigh Anne with me way back in high school, but I always knew he regretted that. I spent the past three years trying to make him see that there was nothing to regret. That I was just as good as her. But even before she came back here, I felt the truth of his love for her somewhere deep inside.

When she returned to Fairhope, it was like the last straw between Preston and me. Even when he was kissing me, I knew the fire had gone out.

And I was helpless to get it back.

Leigh Anne might have met and fallen in love with someone else, but I think something about seeing her again and realizing what he'd lost made Preston start searching for something beyond what I could give him.

Yet here I am, nearly six months later, still clinging to what we had. Wishing I could make him love me.

I start the car and head back toward my apartment, a sadness hanging heavy in my heart. I feel hopeless. Completely lost.

I think there's been a part of me that was still hoping he'd see the light and come back to me. Even after three weeks of not talking, I guess some irrational hope still lingered. Like maybe he would see me across the quad and realize he'd made a terrible mistake.

But seeing him with someone else broke the last of that hope. It's really over between us.

I swipe at a falling tear as I zip the car into my parking spot in front of the small apartment on the east end of campus. All I want to do is go inside, take an aspirin and crawl into bed.

The TV is on in Monica's room, so I sneak past and close my door behind me. But when I go to set my things down on my bed, I notice a large garment bag spread across it.

My stomach twists.

Fuck.

How could I have forgotten?

I throw my bag and coat on the floor and carefully unzip the white garment bag. I pull the red dress out and hold it up, barely able to breathe.

It's strapless with a tight ruched bodice adorned with white pearls under the bust. The skirt flares out just above the knee. A beautiful lace pattern is hand-stitched along a split in the fabric where it ruffles and hitches up, revealing a layer of white lace underneath.

It's my dream dress. Ordered nearly seven months ago from a very expensive boutique in Atlanta specifically for this year's Christmas Memories Charity Ball. The ball is an event Preston's mother throws every year at her house. I had planned on going with Preston and if I'm being honest, when I saw this dress, I had a distinct mental image of me wearing it with him kneeling at my feet, a ring stretched up toward me.

I move in front of the mirror and hold the dress up against my body. I adore this dress, but of all moments for it to arrive, now is just about the worst possible one.

My mother yelled at me when she found out how much I'd spent on it. I had to put it on layaway, making payments once a month to slowly pay it off, but at the time, I was certain it was an investment in my future.

The perfect dress for the perfect night.

I can't bear to look at it anymore.

I slip it back inside the bag and zip it up, then push it to the back of my closet. The dress has already been altered specifically for me, so they won't take it back now. I'd rather just hide it away where I won't have to look at it and think about what might have been.

CHAPTER 4

I go into the bathroom to wash my face and as I remove the bandage, I gasp at the swollen purple cut underneath. I look hideous.

My face crumples in tears and I let them flow. I wrinkle my forehead and the cut stings as it stretches and breaks open. A few drops of warm, sticky blood trickle down the line of my eyebrow. I grab some tissues and press them against the wound, my chest hitching with each sob.

My life is a complete mess. I don't want to live like this anymore.

The door to my bathroom opens and Monica steps inside. When I look up, her face falls and she comes to sit beside me on the cold tile floor.

"What in the world happened?" she asks. She puts a hand on my leg and studies my eye. "I was about to come in here and bitch you out for sneaking in without saying hi, but now I'm going to yell at you for not telling me you were hurt. What did you do?"

I shrug and sniff, pulling the bloody tissues back. "I ran into a door," I say.

She raises an eyebrow and cocks her head to the side. "Seriously?"

"Yes," I say with a laugh that comes out more like a half-sob. "I was trying to take the shortcut through the Science building and ran right into a door as this guy was pushing it open."

"That asshole," she says. "Did you punch him in the nuts?"

I roll my eyes. "It wasn't his fault. I was the one running."

"I can't believe you went to work like this. What if you have a concussion or something?"

"I don't have a concussion," I say. "The guy who hit me was a med student. He made sure I was okay."

Monica sits back against her heels. "Oh really?"

I roll my eyes and toss the tissue toward the trashcan. I miss and have to scoot forward to pick it up again.

"Was he cute?" she asks.

I wipe my face off and stand up, avoiding her eyes. "I guess," I say, not wanting to admit to her that I thought he was gorgeous. I'm too busy being sad and pathetic to let one ounce of possible happiness in the door.

She stands up and peers over my shoulder, studying my face in the mirror. "It doesn't look so bad," she says, but she's grimacing as she says it.

"Liar."

She turns around and leans against the edge of the cabinet. "Is that all that's wrong?" she asks. "You were crying pretty hard."

I close my eyes, so incredibly tired of crying all the time.

I barely even recognize myself anymore. I've become one of those pathetic women who cry at the drop of a hat and never get over the one that got away. If I'm destined to be sad and lonely for the rest of my life, I'd rather the rest of my life only last about five more minutes.

"I saw him," I say.

"Preston?"

I nod. "I don't think he saw me, thank God," I say. "Especially after seeing how bad this cut looks."

"You're gorgeous," Monica says, rubbing my arm. "Even with the cut."

I try to smile, but can't really manage it. "He was talking to some girl," I say. "I didn't recognize her, but there was something in his expression that really got to me. He was into her. I could tell."

Monica sighs.

"I mean, I guess I knew it was bound to happen eventually," I say. "I wasn't expecting him to stay single forever. But still. It sucks so hard." And here come the waterworks again. Anger rushes through me along with fresh tears. "I just want to go to sleep and never wake up."

"Fuck that," Monica says. She grabs my shoulders and turns my body toward her. "Bailey, listen to me. That's bullshit and you know it. I don't ever want to hear something like that come out of your mouth again."

I swallow, my eyes wide. There's real anger in her voice.

"Come on," she says. She stomps out of the bathroom and I follow her toward my closet. "We're going out."

I groan. "Mon, I really don't want to go out tonight," I say. The thought of having to act happy in a crowd of people makes me feel sick to my stomach. "Hello? Concussion?"

"You said you don't have a concussion," she says. She goes through my closet one hanger at a time, evaluating each piece in an instant and moving it to the side with determined fury.

"Well, I still don't feel that great. I have a pounding headache."

"Go into the kitchen and grab some aspirin or something. Drink some water," she says. "We're going out and you're going to have fun. I refuse to let you give up on life because of a man."

I don't go into the kitchen. Instead, I collapse onto my bed and crawl under my blanket. "I'd rather stay here."

"And do what? Lay in bed crying and feeling sorry for yourself? What exactly is that going to accomplish other than making you feel worse?" she says. She puts a hand on her hip. "You're in a danger-zone here, Bailey. If you don't at least try to snap out of this depression and sadness, it's going to swallow you whole. Preston Wright is not the only man alive. He's not even the best man alive. You have to find a way to start seeing past him to all the other possibilities for your future."

I pull the blanket over my head.

"Throw yourself into your paintings," she says, her voice getting louder. "Create something new for yourself. Go out. Make new friends and get rid of those stuck-up richies who haven't called you in weeks. Sleep with six different guys in a week if that's what it takes. I don't care. Anything but laying in this bed all day letting the depression steal your soul."

I curl into a tight ball, terrified of what she's saying, but knowing she's right.

"I'm begging you," she says after a few moments of

silence, her voice softening as she sits at the edge of the bed. "Just come out with me tonight. If you're having the worst time of your life, we can come home. But I need you to at least try. The deeper you let this pull you down, the harder it's going to be to ever recover. Trust me, I've seen it with my own eyes."

Slowly, I sit up and let the blanket fall away from my face. She's talking about her mother now. Her parents divorced when Monica was young and her dad took off to god-knows-where, leaving her mom to raise three kids by herself. Only, her mother never really got over her broken heart. She suffered from depression most of her life and finally succumbed to it, taking her own life just five years ago when Monica was in high school.

Until now, it hadn't occurred to me why Monica was so determined to help me get over this. Why she was pushing me so hard. But now I get it.

I've been so wrapped up in my own sorrow, I couldn't see how this was affecting her.

"Okay," I say, placing my hand on hers. "But promise we can at least go someplace dark where no one will notice I look like I was in a violent fight with a badger."

Monica laughs and throws her arms around me. "Thank you," she says.

I stand up and go to my closet.

"What color looks good with a black eye?"

CHAPTER 5

After a quick dinner and a couple of starter drinks back at the apartment, Monica and I start walking toward the boardwalk. Our apartment is only a few blocks away from the busy strip of shops, restaurants and bars along the beach. It's the perfect location and after turning twenty-one earlier this year, we both had big plans for spending most of our weekends down at the bars, taking in the ocean views while sipping on cocktails.

Sadly, it's mostly been Monica walking down here with some of our other friends.

"It's about time you came down here with me," she says.

"Of course, I have to choose the coldest damn night of the year to walk to the beach." I shiver and pull my scarf tighter around my neck. I left my gloves back at the apartment, and my hands are freezing. "Do you think anyone will even be out? They're saying there's actually a chance of snow this weekend."

"Snow in Georgia? At the beach?" She laughs. "I wouldn't count on it."

I shrug and look up at the night sky. The clouds are low and look white from the lights of the boardwalk shining up toward them.

"Besides," she says. "It's the last weekend before finals and people will be leaving to go home soon for the holidays. Everyone will be out."

My stomach tightens as I think about Preston and the blond mystery chick. What are the odds I might run into him tonight?

I swallow down the worry and press on, determined to prove to Monica that I'm at least making an effort.

As we walk, I concentrate on the pretty decorations. Wreaths, silver bells, red ribbons. It's beautiful out here.

Christmas has always been my favorite time of year, but I've barely even noticed it this year.

My mother always says that Christmas is a season for hope. As Monica and I make our way to the nightclub near the pier, I send a prayer up toward the stars that hope will somehow find its way to me.

CHAPTER 6

"Another," Monica says, motioning to the bartender.

He nods and pours two more shots.

I breathe in deep and grab the glass off the counter. I lift it high, turning toward her on my bar stool. "Here's to moving forward."

"Damn straight," she says. She clinks her glass against mine and we both throw them back.

The Jager is both sweet and bitter as it hits my tongue. The licorice flavor puckers the sides of my mouth, and I swallow it down fast. My throat burns for an instant and then my belly warms.

My head spins with a feeling of sweet surrender. God, I haven't felt like this in weeks. Maybe months. It's like the second I decided to have a good time, something inside me switched on. I feel dangerous, like I'm capable of anything tonight.

Like I'm capable of being anyone.

Right now, I'm tired of being Bailey. I'm so incredibly

tired of being the one constantly doubting where I'm heading or how anyone feels about me. I'm done with it always feeling like I'm not good enough. All of that pain is too damn heavy. I can't carry it anymore or I'm going to fall so far down inside myself that I'll never come up again.

Monica slams her empty glass down on the counter and grabs my hand. "Let's dance."

I hook my feet around the bottom of the bar stool and try to pull away. Okay, so maybe I don't feel as free as I thought.

"Huh-uh. No freaking way," I say.

I look toward the dance floor. It's a mass of sweaty bodies grinding together in the pulsing lights. Mostly couples. I don't need that kind of pressure right now.

"You said you were up for anything tonight," she reminds me. "Stop being so scared to be happy, dammit."

I pout. "I'm here, right? Isn't that a start?"

"It's not enough," she says. "Come on."

She offers her hand to me again and I stare down at it, my heart racing. I don't know why it's so scary for me. It's been so long since I was in a place like this without Preston to hold onto.

I'm so used to sitting alone on nights he didn't want to go out. I centered my entire life around Preston Wright, and I don't know how to live it without him.

I look into Monica's eyes and I can see she's almost reached her limit with me.

She's fed up, and I get it. I do.

A nervous ball of energy forms under my ribs. My heart beats against my chest. I bite the inside of my lip. Why is this so hard? Wasn't I just thinking I felt fearless? How can I go back to being scared a heartbeat later? It's almost as if there are two versions of myself fighting inside of me. One is scared and clings to the past. The other is desperate to change and find happiness.

I swallow, then take her hand.

She screams and throws her free hand over her head. "Yes! Let's do this," she shouts.

I laugh and slip off the stool. We weave our way through the crowd of dancers, the music thumping hard and the lights swirling in my vision.

We stop somewhere in the middle of all these people. At first, I'm hesitant. Awkward. I move my body to the music, but I'm composed and completely out of my element. I look around at the faces of the people surrounding me. I recognize some of them from classes. A few of them were friends of mine in high school. I wait for them to notice me, half expecting some of them to look at me with that same pity I've been seeing from everyone for weeks.

I'm just the poor dumped ex-girlfriend of the hottest, richest guy in town. I'm no one without him.

But no one looks. No one even notices me.

Monica is easy and free on the dance floor. I watch her, wanting to be more like her. She's not tied down by anything. She's just free to be herself and she's never really cared what anyone thinks of her.

Why can't I be like that?

She opens her eyes and sees me staring at her. She shakes her head and smiles. She grabs my hands and begins to dance with me. I laugh because she's making a fool of herself and she doesn't even care.

She pulls me toward her and shouts in my ear, "Just let it

go, Bailey. Just for one night."

Tears well up in my eyes. She makes it sound so easy. As if healing my heart is only a matter of deciding not to hurt. As if it's just that simple.

And what if it is?

I breath in and out and let the music fill me up. I think about all the weeks of sadness and wonder what it would feel like to let it all go. To choose happiness instead. To be free from the burden of it all.

My body loosens and my movements become more fluid and organic.

I give in to the moment, concentrating on the thumping bass and the sweat rolling down my spine.

I close my eyes and forget that anyone else is here. No one is watching me or judging me. No one is telling me I'm not good enough. I don't have anyone or anything to answer to right now but myself. With every movement, a piece of my shell breaks loose and flakes away.

A tear slides down my cheek, but this time, it's different. I'm not crying from sadness or heartbreak. These tears are coming from a place deep inside that has been clinging to this belief that I'm not worthy of love or friendship. Maybe it's the alcohol. Or maybe it's from seeing Preston flirting with someone new. I don't know. But for some reason, I feel a new me stirring just under the surface of my skin.

My tears begin to fall harder and faster.

The more I break free, the more I begin to sob. I can't breathe.

I turn and run, pushing my way through the crowd. I think I hear Monica shout my name, but I don't look back.

I run straight toward the back door and bolt out into the

alleyway behind the club.

As soon as the door closes behind me, I double over, clutching my stomach. I lean back against the brick wall, sobs shaking my body.

I let all those things I haven't wanted to admit to myself pour through me. I let them come to the surface and I face them, finally understanding that my worst fears have all come true. The whole time I was with Preston, I felt like such a fraud. I never felt that I belonged in that group of friends with their expensive clothes and their privileged lives. I always felt lesser and everything I did—every choice I made along the way—was about pleasing them or trying to be one of them.

But now I know the truth.

I never really did belong. If those people had been my real friends, they would have rallied around me when Preston broke things off. Instead, I haven't heard a single word from Summer or Krystal in weeks. Without Preston, I'm nothing to them.

And deep down, I always knew it was true.

I wipe the waterfall of tears from my cheeks and chest, breathing deeply as my sobs begin to calm. I'm sure by now all of the makeup I put on earlier is completely gone. My eyes feel puffy and raw. But I feel different. Purged.

A tingle spreads through my body, as if something has shifted for me. As if the universe is trying to tell me something big is right around the corner.

Just then, the back door swings open and someone steps out, a cell phone clutched in his hand.

I glance up and my breath catches in my throat.

Judd.

CHAPTER 7

I stand there like a deer caught in headlights.

He lifts his cell phone to his ear, then turns and sees me. His lips part and for a brief moment, we're two statues. Then, slowly, his lips curl into a smile that makes my heart skip a beat.

Judd's hand falls to his side, his call forgotten.

"Bailey," he says.

"Judd." I raise my hand in a salute, then feel stupid.

He shakes his head. "Twice in one day," he says. "Lucky."

My hands tingle. "Lucky for you, maybe." I point to the gash on my head.

He laughs. "I really am sorry about that," he says. "Can I buy you a drink to make it up to you?"

He hitches his thumb back toward the door.

I glance toward the door. "Sure, why not?"

He puts his phone back into his pocket, then pushes his hair behind his ears. His face is freshly shaved and when he moves, I catch the scent of him on the wind. Instead of the worn jeans he was wearing earlier, he's changed into a pair of dark jeans that hug the muscles in his thighs. His dark navy button-up shirt is open slightly at the top, showing off the smooth chest beneath.

"Did you need to make a call?" I ask.

He opens the door and the music spills out into the alley. "It's not important," he says. "What were you doing out here, anyway?"

I laugh, knowing he has to notice my red eyes and tear-stained face. I probably have raccoon eyes from my mascara at this point. If he still wants to buy me a drink after seeing me cry twice in one day, this guy's insane. "I was having an epiphany," I say.

"Oh really," he says. He gives me that smile again. That half-smile that makes him look like he has a secret. A sexy secret I'm dying to know. "What kind of epiphany?"

"Buy me that drink and maybe I'll tell you."

Judd leads me toward the bar. We sit down on a corner so that our bar stools are facing each other instead of just side-by-side. I want to hide my face. I have to look horrible. At least Monica stayed true to her promise and brought me to a dark place.

"What do you want?" Judd asks. He motions toward the bartender and orders a beer for himself.

Out of habit, I order a Jack and coke. It's my go-to drink when I'm with Preston. He made a joke once that I was more fun when I was drinking Jack Daniels, so I started ordering it all the time. I don't even really like it that much. All I've cared about for the past three years is whether Preston wanted me to like something.

"Wait," I call out to the bartender. He grabs Judd's beer from the cooler and walks back toward us.

"Can I get something else instead?"

"Of course, you want another shot of Jagermeister?"

I shake my head. I don't even know what to order. I just know I don't care if I never have another Jack and coke in my life. "What can you make that's Christmas-y? Something strong that tastes good."

Out of the corner of my eye, I see Judd raise an eyebrow at the word strong. He takes a quick drink of his beer. "Sounds like you have your work cut out for you, Beau."

"I think I have just the thing," Beau says. "If you don't like it, I'll make you something else."

"Do you guys know each other?" I ask Judd when the bartender walks away.

Judd nods. "Yeah, he's one of my good buddies. I hang out here on the weekends when I'm not working in the lab or studying," he says. "Sometimes he slips me free drinks. It's a perk of being friends with a bartender."

"Ah," I say, swiveling on my stool. "So when you said you'd buy me a drink, what you meant was that you'd buy me a free drink?"

He cuts his eyes toward me and one side of his lips curls into a smile, that I have to say gets my heart racing a little bit. How did I miss how good looking this guy is?

"Maybe," he says. "Dating on a budget 101. Find a bar where you can get free drinks."

I laugh. Dating on a budget was never in Preston's vocabulary. He spent money like it grew on trees. I guess for him it really kind of does.

Still, the fact that Judd just used the word 'dating' sends a funny jolt through my mid-section.

When Beau comes back, he's carrying a bright green drink in a martini glass, garnished with a red cherry.

"Wow, this looks amazing," I say. "What's in it?"

"Vodka and Midori," Beau says.

I take a sip and am instantly addicted. "I can't even taste the alcohol in this."

"Exactly the point," he says. He winks at Judd, then takes off to help a group of girls who just hobbled over from the dance floor.

"What was that wink about? Are you trying to get me drunk?" I tease.

Judd throws up his hands. "I didn't say that," he says. "It just seems like you've had the kind of day where you could really benefit from a couple of drinks."

My smile fades and I play with the cherry. "Is it that obvious?"

"That you've had a bad day?" he asks. "Other than the fact that you've got a nasty cut on your forehead from some jerk hitting you in the face with a door, you were just standing in the alley of a nightclub crying. I'd say, yeah, it's pretty obvious."

Part of me wants to get up and walk away. What kind of guy tells you straight out that you look like hell and could use a drink? Then again, other than Monica, not many people in my life are willing to tell it like it is. Most of the people I know have been tiptoeing around me like I was a ticking time-bomb ever since Preston broke up with me. No one wants to push me or really talk to me about what I've been going through.

This guy doesn't seem to have any trouble just cutting through the bullshit and talking about the obvious.

He's very different from Preston, and right now, that's exactly what I'm looking for.

One glance at the dance floor tells me Monica's going to be here for a while. She's dancing with some guy I don't recognize. And calling what they're doing dancing is really a stretch, considering they're mostly just grinding each other.

I may as well sit here and enjoy myself. What could a few more drinks hurt?

"So, Judd, there's something I've been wanting to ask you since this afternoon," I say.

He takes another drink and my eyes drift to his mouth as it touches the glass. My stomach flips and I force my eyes away.

"Ask me anything," he says.

I look down at the napkin and fiddle with a small plastic straw. It's been years since I looked at anyone and felt that first flutter of excitement and attraction. Either this is the greatest drink ever invented or there might really be something here.

I almost lose my train of thought in my nervousness.

"Why do I feel like I've seen you somewhere before?" I ask. "You look familiar, but I can't remember ever meeting you before."

He laughs. "The Cup," he says. "I come in there a lot to study."

My eyes widen and I study him. "Caramel mocha," I say, snapping my fingers. "I knew I recognized you from somewhere."

How in the heck did I not notice how amazing and sexy

he is before now? Was I really so blinded by Preston that I missed something that was right in front of my eyes?

Or is the alcohol going straight to my crotch?

Judd downs the rest of his beer and taps the bar top twice. Beau sets another down a few seconds later, like this is something they do all the time.

"You don't strike me as a med student," I say, taking another sip of this magical green cocktail.

"Why?" He chuckles.

I shrug. "Long, impossible hours. No time for fun," I say. "Plus, you don't look the type."

I honestly don't know why I'm saying all this. The alcohol is making my head spin and there doesn't seem to be a filter between my brain and my mouth at the moment.

He leans closer. "It's the hair right?"

I nod and look him over. "Yeah, maybe a little," I say. "And the shoes."

He cocks his head toward me. "Shoes?"

"I know it's stupid, but I've always thought a person's shoes said a lot about their character. Their ambitions, if you will. And you're wearing those beat-up tennis shoes with a hole in them," I say. "I would have guessed you more of an anthropology major or something. Maybe psych. Something more liberal arts than medical."

"Oh really?" he says. "I never considered guessing some-one's major by their shoes, but I'll have to try it some time."

He looks down and I realize he's looking at my shoes. I giggle and turn, holding my legs out straight so he can see my shoes clearly.

"What's your best guess?"

I'm wearing a pair of red heels that are just barely

covered by the cuff of my dark blue jeans. I almost always wear heels when I go out. Otherwise, I'm super short compared to everyone else around me. Besides, Preston is tall and he always liked for me to wear heels, so I always did. I have a closet full of them.

Judd brings a hand to his face, rubbing his chin and looking serious. I can't help but laugh at his intense study of my red heels.

"Red shoes are very complex," he says. His eyes travel all the way up my legs and he takes his time. My body heats up at his intense look. "They say you're daring and not afraid to be yourself. Red heels definitely say confident and classy, but with a touch of rebel."

I laugh, but not because he's right. I laugh because he's so far off, he's not even in the right zip code. I may act confident, but the truth is that I'm terrified of being myself. I've spent the majority of my life in a constant state of worry about what other people will think of me.

"Education or maybe something like Communications," he says finally.

"Which one?" I say. "You can only choose one."

"Definitely Education, then," he says. "You've got that sexy teacher vibe about you."

Warmth spreads up my neck and cheeks. He thinks I'm sexy? I can't even remember the last time someone called me that.

"Wrong on both counts," I say. "Art."

He slaps his hand down on the bar top. "Damn," he says. "That was my third guess."

I laugh. "Liar."

He looks at me and winks. His smile is so free and

genuine it tears at me. Pulls me toward him. He lights up when he laughs.

"That explains the paint, I guess," he says.

I hold my hands out, studying my fingers. I try to keep my nails short, but I always end up with paint or clay or something under my fingernails.

"Good eye," I say. The fact that he noticed the paint even in the darkness of this place impresses me.

"Something like that," he says. "Want another drink?"

A buzz of energy flares through my body. I want to know this guy. It's such a foreign feeling, I don't even know what to do with it.

I look toward the dance floor and see that Monica is standing at the edge of the crowd staring at me, her mouth open in shock. She catches my eye and jumps up and down like a little girl. She raises her fist into the air and heads back onto the dance floor.

I laugh and shake my head, then turn back to Judd.

I said I wanted something to bring hope to the season. I said I felt the universe was trying to tell me something. How can this all be a coincidence? Maybe it's fate.

And who am I to deny fate?

Without taking my eyes off of his, I reach out and tap the bar top twice.

CHAPTER 8

Several rounds of drinks later, my head is spinning. For the first time in weeks, I'm actually having fun. Judd is smart and sexy and he makes me laugh.

We talk about school and our favorite movies and music. It's so amazing to just let loose and be myself around a guy. I can't even remember the last time I talked about myself so freely or had someone who seemed genuinely interested in what I have to say.

With every drink, my lips become a little looser and my inhibitions fade.

"If someone walked up right now and offered you two tickets to any concert in the world, who would you go see?" I ask.

Beau sets another drink down in front of me and I transfer my straw from my empty to the new one. I'm not sure how many of these I've had, but I'm pretty sure at this point, it's one too many.

I'm not about to push it away, though. I like this version of me.

"Do they have to be alive?" Judd asks, then tosses back the last of his beer.

I squint my eyes, thinking. "Yes," I say. "Wait, no. Living or dead. Best, most amazing concert of your life. Who would it be?"

"The Beatles," he says. "Hands down, no contest."

My eyes widen. "The Beatles are my life," I say. "What year? Early years Beatles or Abbey Road Beatles?"

"Abbey Road," he says, lifting a single eyebrow. "Stupid question."

Abbey Road is my favorite album on the planet and the fact that he just gave that answer makes me want to crawl across the bar and kiss him.

Without thinking, I grab his hand. "You are my soul mate," I say.

An electricity passes between us when we touch. His eyes meet mine and time stands still for one long moment. My heart races inside my chest, and I'm so in love with this feeling I don't ever want it to end.

I've spent so many years doing everything to try to keep Preston interested in me that I forgot what it was like to feel this way about someone. I forgot that there might be other guys on this planet who might be worth spending time with.

"Let's dance," I say. I slide off my chair and pull him toward me.

I expect him to act like Preston always does, refusing to dance and acting like I'm stupid for wanting him on the dance floor.

But he doesn't. Judd smiles and stands, walking with me hand-in-hand to the dance-floor.

I stumble a little, my sense of balance totally screwed from all the vodkas. Judd reaches to steady me and as his strong arms circle my waist, my breath catches. I press my body close to his and start moving to the music.

The song is fast, but we move slowly at first, exploring those first tentative touches.

He presses his palms flat against my lower back, pulling me closer.

I lift my hands to his arms and run them slowly from his elbow up his bicep, electrified by the feel of his skin against mine. I look into his eyes as I touch him, letting my fingers explore every ripple of muscle.

Something deep inside me responds and my whole body grows warm and eager. Any inhibitions and sadness I felt on this dance-floor a few hours ago are gone, replaced by a desire that rocks me to my core.

Who the hell is this guy? And where has he been all my life?

Right now, I'm not even thinking about the future. I just want him right now. I want this. And in my drunken haze, I feel so incredibly attracted to him, I suddenly wish we were in a more private place so I could explore more of him than just his biceps.

My mouth is so dry, I can barely swallow. I let my lips part slightly so I can breathe and his gaze dips to them. Desire flashes in his eyes and it makes me feel beautiful. Brave.

I want to kiss him, but the raw, sudden need for it scares the crap out of me. What am I doing?

I lower my hands and pull away slightly, not knowing exactly what I want. Or what I should want.

I close my eyes and lose myself to the music instead. A new song begins and the bass is thumping hard. I let myself go, feeling free after so many weeks of feeling hopeless and broken.

I turn around, pressing my back to his. We move together, our bodies pressed close. Judd's hand circles around my waist, resting at the spot where my shirt meets the band of my jeans. Sometimes when I move, his thumb brushes the bare skin on my stomach. Every touch of his skin is like fire against me, burning me up.

Sweat trickles down my back. I left my hair down tonight and it's so long, it falls all the way down my back to my waist. After a few dances, it's so hot, I have to reach up and pull it away from my neck. I gather it all into a bun high up on my head.

Behind me, Judd blows cool air on my neck and I shiver.

I turn around and he swallows as I lift my eyes to his.

I'm breathless, wanting him and completely helpless to deny it. I don't know if it's the alcohol or the look in his eyes, but I don't care. I just want to lose myself in this feeling of being wanted.

I place one hand on his chest and his lips part. I grab his shirt into my fist and pull him down toward me. Our eyes are locked the entire time, as if we're the only two people here.

His eyes close just before his lips reach mine. I lift up just slightly on my tiptoes, closing that last breath between us. And when his lips meet mine, a fire erupts between us.

I can't breathe. I can't think. My body is reduced to fire and need. My fist tightens and I lean into his kiss.

His mouth opens, asking for more, and I obey. I open to him and our kiss becomes a conversation. A question and response. A give and take.

His hand grips my hips, squeezing and tugging me closer.

Below my waist, I feel my body respond to his touch. I grind my hips against his, gasping as he hardens against me.

At the edge of my mind, I'm aware of the fact that we're in a room of people, but I don't care. I couldn't force myself away from him if I wanted to.

Beneath my fist, his chest rises and falls with each heavy breath. I feel the rumble of a groan even though the music's too loud for me to hear it. I loosen my grip on his shirt and let my hands find their way around his neck. I run my fingers through his hair and he sucks in a breath and pulls away.

When he looks down at me, his hazel eyes are intense and deep with need. We're both breathing fast and hard, our bodies no longer moving to the music. We're statues, pressed tight, wanting more but not wanting to move away from this moment.

He leans his forehead against mine and we work to catch our breath.

My heart vibrates in my chest and I know with absolute certainty that I want him. I've never had a one-night-stand before, but I've never wanted anyone as much as I want him right now.

I want this night to last forever.

I lift up, getting close enough that he can hear me over the thumping of the music. "Let's get out of here," I say. "I want to go home with you tonight."

I've never spoken so boldly to anyone before and when his body tenses, fear zings through me.

He steps backward, untangling himself from my embrace. His forehead is wrinkled with tension, and I stare up at him, questioning.

He reaches for my hand and I give it to him, not sure exactly what he's thinking. He leads me back toward the bar where the music's not quite as loud, but he doesn't sit back down. Instead, he throws a twenty dollar bill on the counter and waves to Beau.

I think he's going to take me back to his place, but as soon as we step out into the cool night air, he pauses. He's not acting like a guy who knows he's about to get laid.

I swallow, nervous. The last thing I need right now is to get rejected, especially after falling all over him.

But I already know it's coming. I can feel it in the way the air between us has changed. More rejection. Oh god, what have I done? I never should have come out tonight.

"Bailey, I really like you," he starts.

I pull my hand away from his and turn away. Tears spring to my eyes. I'm mortified. I just want to run away. I don't want to face this.

"Hey wait," he says. He rushes around to stand in front of me, putting his hands on my shoulders. "Listen, I mean it, Bailey. I like you so much."

"But?"

He runs a hand through his shoulder-length hair. "But I don't want to ruin this by sleeping with you the first night."

I shake my head and start walking. "I get it," I say.

"Where are you going?" he asks, jogging to catch up with me. "Hold on a second. Let me walk you home."

I stop, feeling like such a fool. "Don't bother, okay?"

"Why are you getting so angry?" he asks. "I thought we had a good time tonight."

"I did too," I say. "That's why I wanted to go home with you. I didn't want it to end. But apparently you did. I get it. You don't want me."

He laughs and it stings. I keep walking.

"Bailey, come on," he says. He grabs my hand and pulls me back toward him. "It's not that I don't want you, believe me. You have to know that. Kissing you just now?" He sighs and searches the air above my head, then looks back into my eyes. "God, that was just about the most amazing kiss in the history of kisses. But we've been drinking. A lot. I'm not going to take advantage of you."

My heart aches. If kissing me was so amazing, why doesn't he want more?

"It isn't taking advantage if I want it too," I say.

He shakes his head. "It doesn't matter," he says. "I'm not that kind of guy, Bailey. Believe me, I do want you. You have to know that."

"Forget it," I say, yanking my hand from his. "I'm going home."

Even though I'm drunk, I'm partly aware that I'm irrationally angry. I don't even understand why I'm so mad. All I know is that I wanted him and I needed this tonight. I wanted to feel beautiful. I wanted to feel wanted. And rejecting me now just ruined everything.

He calls my name again, but I don't turn around. I just keep walking.

I stumble slightly in my heels, but catch myself before I fall. I stop and yank the shoes off my feet. I throw them down onto the paved path and just leave them there.

When I glance behind me, I see him pick up my shoes and keep walking.

"Bailey," he says.

I lift my hand, not turning around. "Leave me alone," I say. "Just leave me the fuck alone."

I walk all the way back to my apartment without turning around again. Still, I can feel him behind me. It takes me a couple of tries to get the key into the lock, but when I finally do, I push my door open and turn to close it, catching a glimpse of Judd standing in the parking lot below, holding two red shoes.

CHAPTER 9

The alarm jerks me from my sleep.

I moan and slam the snooze button. I sink deeper under the covers, hiding my eyes from the sun shining through my windows.

My head pounds and my eyelids feel sticky and heavy.

The memory of last night comes flooding back and I curl into a ball under the covers. My stomach gurgles and I press my lips together tightly, waiting for the wave of nausea to pass.

I can't even remember the last time I had so much to drink.

What was I thinking?

I pull my pillow over my head, wanting to hide from the realization that I made such a fool of myself with Judd last night. We were having such a great time, and I completely ruined it. One kiss and I was ready to jump into bed with him? I bet he thinks I'm a complete idiot.

He'll probably never talk to me again, and I wouldn't blame him.

My door clicks as it opens and I groan into the pillow. "Go away."

"Good morning, sunshine," Monica says. She yanks the covers off my body and snatches the pillow out of my hands.

I sit up and reach for the comforter, but she smacks my hand.

"No way are you going to avoid me this morning," she says. "Especially not after you abandoned me at the club last night."

I scoot toward the headboard and pull my other pillow into my lap. Monica has a steaming cup of coffee in her hand and she offers it to me.

"Thanks," I say. "And I'm sorry about last night. I don't know what got into me."

"Apparently a tall, sexy guy with long, dark blond hair," she says, a sparkle in her eyes. She sits down across from me, tucking her legs under her slim frame. "Tell me everything."

I lean my head back against the wall. "You don't want to know."

"I half expected him to be here when I opened the door," she says.

"Then why did you come in without knocking?" I throw the pillow at her. "You perv."

She ducks and the pillow sails past. "Hey, if you have a chance to see a guy like that with his shirt off, you take it, okay?" she says with a laugh.

"You are so bad," I say. "I'm so sorry to disappoint you."

"What happened, then? You guys were looking very into each other on the dance floor, if I remember correctly," she says. "And what the hell is up with your shoes on our doorstep this morning?"

"This morning?" I ask, raising an eyebrow. "Does that mean you just got home?"

She shrugs and tries to hide her smile.

"You slut," I joke.

"Hey, you're one to talk," she says. "I saw you kissing him. Who was that guy? He was freaking h-o-t."

I sink deeper, pulling my legs up to my chest. "His name is Judd," I say. "He's a med student who comes into The Cup sometimes."

She gives me a sideways look. "Why haven't you mentioned him before?"

"I honestly barely noticed him before."

"How is that even possible?" she asks. "If that guy walked into Amerigo's, I would make a beeline for that table and spend the whole night at his beck and call."

I roll my eyes, wishing I had an extra pillow to throw at her.

"Well, I ruined it, so it doesn't matter anyway."

"What do you mean? He seemed very into you the last time I saw you guys. I assumed you left together," she says.

"We sort of did," I say. "But I was such an idiot, Mon. I mean, we were having an awesome time and then we started dancing together. I thought there was something there between us. I had way too much to drink, I guess, because I pretty much threw myself at him."

"I don't think he minded," she says with a giggle.

"I didn't either, at first. But then I asked him to take me home." I cringe as the words leave my mouth. I've never done anything like that in my life, and I have no idea why I chose last night to start.

"And?"

"And what? He said no," I say with a shrug. "End of story."

"Wait, you guys spend hours talking at the bar, you kiss like crazy on the dance floor, and then he tells you that no, he isn't interested in taking you home and ravaging your body? Okay, so he's crazy."

"No, I'm stupid," I say. "He was probably just being nice to me after hitting me in the face with a door and—"

"Whoa, wait a second," she says, holding up her hand. "He's the one who hit you with the door?"

"Yes," I say, lifting my hand to the sore spot above my eye. It's still tender and I suck in a breath. "Classy, huh?"

"It's cute," she says. "Not the cut, but the story. So he comes into your cafe to study and hang out sometimes and then he just happens to hit you with a door? And then somehow, he also just happens to be at the same club we were last night? It sounds like fate to me."

"Shut up," I say, not wanting to tell her how close she is to being right. "It's not fate. It's...I don't know. Coincidence. A very embarrassing coincidence. I'm sure next time he sees me, he'll run the other way."

She reaches out and squeezes my foot. "Don't say that," she says. "Besides, maybe he was just trying to be a gentleman. Maybe he doesn't put out on the first date."

I can't help but smile. Monica always knows how to make me feel better, but I think this situation is kind of hopeless. "What guy says no to a hot girl who is throwing herself at him?"

She stares at me, her mouth slightly open.

"See? No one," I say. "The only guy that says no is a guy who either isn't interested or who, I don't know, is saving himself for marriage or something. And he doesn't strike me as the type."

"What about the kiss?" she asks. "Did he kiss you? Or did you kiss him?"

I close my eyes and absently touch my lips. "I kissed him," I say. "But he kissed me back. He was into it. Or at least I thought he was. There's no way I imagined that. There was something there between us. What if I've been out of the game so long, I just imagined that he was into it? What if he was just being nice?"

"Kissing you passionately just to be nice? I don't think so."

I laugh. "Yeah, maybe not," I say. I take a few more sips of the coffee, my headache easing up. "I don't know, then. Maybe he's dating someone else. Or maybe he's just not really that into me and didn't want to take it any further than a fun night at the club."

Even as I say it, though, I don't think it's true.

"But the thing is, even before the kiss, we were having such a great time." I clasp the warm mug between both hands. "We connected, you know? He even loved the same music I do. It was crazy. I never really talked to Preston like that and we were together for years. He never asked me about what kind of music I like or what kind of movies I wanted to watch. And even if he did, I was always so scared to tell him the truth. I always told Preston what he wanted to hear, thinking that if I was the perfect girlfriend, eventually he'd really love me."

I fall silent. I've never put words to it like that, but as soon as they come out of my mouth, I am hit with the absolute truth of them.

With Preston, I was always fighting to feel worthy of him. Last night with Judd, I was just myself. And for a little while, I thought that was enough.

Monica pulls me into a hug. "Honey, if Preston couldn't see that you were already perfect just the way you are, then he never deserved you anyway."

Tears spring to my eyes. "I'm not sure I ever really gave him the chance to see the real me," I say, realizing it for the first time.

"Then it's his loss," she says.

"Is it?" I say, wiping at my eyes.

"Absolutely," she says. "And if Judd doesn't see it either, then screw him."

"I tried," I say with a smile.

Monica laughs and stands up. "I'm sure you did," she says. She turns and stares down at me. "It's really good to see you smile again. I really missed that happy face."

"Me too," I say.

"Now get your hungover ass out of bed and get ready for work," she says. "You're gonna be late."

I lean forward to get a better look at the clock beside my bed. It's nine-thirty and my shift at The Cup starts in thirty minutes. "Shit," I say. I jump out of bed and run toward the shower without the luxury of time to worry about last night for another minute.

CHAPTER 10

I'm halfway through my shift when the bell over the door rings.

I look up and hazel eyes meet mine. My heart skips a beat and my mouth falls open slightly.

I stop in mid-step, a very full cup of cappuccino in one hand and a hot chocolate in the other.

Sassy, one of the other servers, comes around the corner in a rush and smacks right into me. Coffee and hot chocolate splash down the front of my white work shirt and I stumble backward, the cups crashing to the ground.

Everyone in the small cafe turns to look. I bend down, avoiding the one set of eyes I don't want watching me right now. How am I constantly making such a fool of myself around him?

"Be careful," Mr. Edwards says. "Here, grab a broom. Don't pick that up by hand. I don't want you to cut yourself, Bailey."

I stand and take the broom from him. My face is growing

hotter by the second. I don't dare look up and see if Judd is still watching me. If he's smart, he turned around and got the hell out of here.

"You okay?" Sassy asks. "I'm sorry, I wasn't watching where I was going."

"I'm fine," I say. "It was my fault. I zoned out for a second. I'm not feeling too great today."

"Do you need to head home early?" Mr. Edwards asks. I hadn't realized he was still standing behind me. "You shouldn't be in here serving if you're coming down with something."

I shake my head and start sweeping up the mess on the floor. I can't afford to take any time off work right now. I paid an arm and a leg for that stupid dress for the Christmas dance. If I don't work my butt off this month, there's no way I'll make rent.

"I'm fine," I say. "I just didn't get much sleep last night."

"Okay, well, get that cleaned up and I'll head back and remake those drinks for you."

"Cappuccino and Hot choc," I say.

Sassy and Mr. Edwards disappear into the small kitchen, leaving me out front to clean up the broken cups.

After about the third pass over the wet floor, a pair of tattered sneakers appears at the edge of the mess. I swallow, my stomach flip-flopping.

"Hey, you okay?"

The sound of his voice sends shivers up my spine. I look up and all I can see are those delicious lips. I look back down, not even wanting to know why he's here today, of all days.

"I'm fine," I say. "Sit anywhere you want. I'll send Sassy

over to take your order."

"Wait—"

But I'm already gone.

I turn the corner out of sight and press my back against the wall. I press the broom and dustpan tight against my body, clutching them so tight. What the heck is he doing here?

I really hope he isn't here to rub last night in my face.

I wonder if I can still get out of work and head home early. I can't really afford it, but I do not want to be here with him for the next hour or two while he sits and studies. There's no way I'll be able to concentrate.

Even if there was some part of him that was coming back to see me today, there's no way he's going to like me more with coffee stains all over my shirt. Besides, there are bags under my eyes and my hair is pulled into a tight bun that was still dripping wet when I left the house this morning.

Not exactly looking my best today.

Besides, Judd already rejected me once. I'm not about to give him the opportunity to do it again.

Mr. Edwards emerges from the kitchen and I spring into action, hoping he doesn't realize I've just been standing here. "All cleaned up?" he asks.

"The floor is," I say.

"I think I have a spare shirt in the closet in my office," he says. "It might be a bit big for you, but it'll work for today. Why don't you run in there and get changed so you don't have to wear that the rest of the day."

I nod and disappear into his office, glad for a temporary escape. I take my time. I hope Sassy gets Judd's order. I don't think I can face him.

He was the last person I expected to see here today. I thought he'd be avoiding this place and anywhere I might be like the plague.

And what the heck is up with the way I reacted just now? Just a moment's glimpse into his eyes rendered me completely paralyzed for a second. I've never reacted to a guy's presence like that in my entire life.

I pull the coffee-stained shirt over my head and toss it on the floor. The manager's extra shirt is hanging on the back of the door. He was right about it being big. It's an extra-large and it swallows me. I try to tuck it in so it looks like an actual shirt instead of a tent, but it's hopeless.

Great. So not only did I proceed to make a complete clown of myself in front of Judd for the second day in a row, but now I also have to look like I'm drowning in white cotton for the rest of the afternoon.

Attractive.

I can't stall in here much longer, and I really don't want to get in any trouble. I need this job.

I grab my dirty shirt from the floor and walk into the hallway. I toss it on top of my backpack and take a deep breath, drudging up any confidence I can force to the surface before I walk out front.

Maybe he didn't stay. Maybe he's gone.

As soon as I come out into the main part of the cafe, my eyes flicker to the table near the window where he always sits. He's there and my shoulders tense.

Judd has his earbuds in and is hunched over a big stack of books.

Before running into him—or running into a door—yesterday, I didn't think I'd ever paid much attention to him.

But watching him now, I realize I've watched him there many times before. He's probably been in here dozens of times. Even though he always sits near the window, he always faces in toward the cafe. Most of the people who sit there choose to face out so they can watch the people walking by. The window has a great view of the quad where students play Frisbee and sit studying in the summer or walk back and forth to classes in the winter.

But it occurs to me now Judd always sits facing in.

As if he senses me staring, he looks up. A slow smile tugs at his lips, but before I can react or do anything other than stare like a dumbass, he goes back to his books.

Sassy walks up to take his order and I feel a strange disappointment wash over me.

What the heck is wrong with me? Wasn't I hoping she would take his order so I wouldn't have to?

I straighten my shoulders and tear my eyes away from his table. Yes, I was hoping she would take his order. I'm sure he's only here because he's used to studying here. Now that I think about it, it's close to the labs, which is where I ran into him yesterday. He probably comes here because it's convenient. It has nothing to do with me.

For the next hour and a half, I stay as far away from his table as I can. Whenever someone comes in and sits near him, I beg Sassy to take their order. I do my best to stay behind the counter and in the kitchen for most of the afternoon.

We close early on Saturdays, and as five approaches, I keep expecting him to leave. But he stays.

And stays.

Every once in a while, I catch him watching me. And

every time that happens, I end up spilling someone's drink or knocking over the salt or tripping over a chair.

If I can't get it together, I'm going to have demand that he leave just so I can get my work done without turning into a walking bruise. At this rate, I'll be fired before the shift is over.

When the last table pays out and leaves, I have no choice but to move close to him and clean the table next to him. It's my turn to close and Sassy left half an hour ago.

My heart thumps against my ribs as I approach the table. I try my best to avoid his eyes, but I can only hold off so long before the magnetic pull of him demands my attention. I glance at him for just the tiniest second.

My hand bumps the half-empty water glass on the table and it knocks over with a clatter. I scramble to catch it, but the water spills over the top and off the side of the table. I collapse into an empty chair and lean my head dramatically against the table.

"I give up," I say.

Judd's laughter rings out in the deserted cafe. I can't help but laugh with him. I've never had a more ridiculous day in my life.

I peek over at him. God, that smile does things to my insides. It lights up his eyes like they're full of magic.

I smile back despite myself. "You're going to have to stop coming in here or I'm going to lose my job," I say.

"Who? Me?" he says, looking around.

I roll my eyes. "You're distracting."

He wiggles his eyebrows and I lift my hands up to hide the smile that's attacked my face.

"You're pretty distracting yourself," he says.

"Yeah, I'm a regular clown," I say. "I could keep people entertained for hours with my clumsiness."

"I wasn't talking about your clumsiness," he says, his voice low and his smile fading into a serious look that makes my breath catch in my throat.

"I wasn't expecting to see you here today," I say. "I figured after last night you'd want to avoid me for the rest of your life."

He shakes his head. "Not a chance," he says. "Besides, you're the one who's been avoiding me all afternoon."

I stand up and start cleaning up the latest mess. I don't know what to say to him. It's true, but only because I thought it would be less embarrassing than having him turn me down yet again.

"Silence," he says. "Does that mean you really have been avoiding me?"

I shrug, not wanting to meet his eyes. "Maybe."

He turns in his chair. "Bailey, I had a great time last night," he says. "I haven't been able to stop thinking about you."

A tingle travels up my spine. "I acted like an idiot last night," I say. "How can you possibly still be interested in me?"

"You were beautiful last night," he says.

"You turned me down."

"And it was one of the hardest things I've ever done," he says. "Trust me, it wasn't because I didn't want you."

Warmth crawls up my neck and cheeks and I look away. "I was afraid I ruined everything when I asked you to take me home with you," I say.

"You didn't ruin anything," he says. "I just didn't want you to wake up in the morning and feel like you'd made a huge mistake. If I ever take you to my bed, I want it to be because you really want to be there. And I don't want you to have any reason to regret it."

I rest my elbow on the table and cover my mouth with my hand. I'm blushing and smiling like a little girl, and I can't hide it. I've never met a guy who was so honest and direct. He doesn't dance around the point. He just says it like it is.

"Will you go out with me?" he asks.

I bite my lower lip and look over at him. "When?"

"Now," he says, straightening.

I shake my head and motion to my outfit. "There's no way I can go out looking like this," I say. "I'm wearing a freaking tent."

"And you look hot in it."

I roll my eyes. "Shut up."

"I'll just call you Barnum & Bailey," he says, laughing. "Look what tents did for them. The Greatest Show on Earth."

I laugh and the sound comes from way down deep inside. It's like medicine to my poor, sad heart.

"Say yes," he says. "I'll take you to dinner."

My face is all smile now. "Someplace dark and casual," I say.

"Deal," he says. "What time do you get off work?"

I look up at the door, then stand and turn the sign over. "Now," I say. "Just let me clean up this last table and cash out. I'll be less than ten minutes."

"It's a date," he says.

I grab the tables and glasses off the table beside him and practically float toward the kitchen.

CHAPTER 11

Judd slings his bag over his shoulder, then reaches for my hand.

As our skin touches, I feel that same pinch of attraction deep down in my belly. We walk together across campus, and I feel like a different version of myself. I've spent the majority of my three years at Fairhope Coastal University as Preston's girlfriend. Not once have I been on a date with a new guy or even so much as touched another guy besides Preston.

It feels foreign and wonderful and new all at the same time.

When I sprinted toward that door yesterday, I never could have imagined it would have brought me to this moment. It's amazing how fast someone can enter your life and start to change everything.

Amazing and terrifying all at once.

"Where are you taking me?" I ask.

I look awful in this shirt. I can't believe he didn't want

me to go home and change. From now on, I vow to always keep a fresh change of clothes in the bottom of my bag.

"I thought maybe we'd walk along the beach for a while," he says. "It's a really nice night out if you're not too cold."

I have my leather jacket on over my work clothes and other than cold cheeks, I feel good. I forgot to bring my gloves, but he's doing a good job keeping one of my hands warm. I have the other shoved deep in my pocket.

"I think I'm fine for a little while," I say. "But I am pretty hungry."

"I've got that covered," he says.

"Okay," I say, assuming he's going to take me to one of the many bars or restaurants near the pier.

He shocks me when he walks up to the hot dog cart on the corner at the end of the boardwalk.

"You can't be serious?"

"What? You don't like hotdogs? You asked for something dark and casual." He elbows me and when I look up, his eyes are dancing in the dim light.

"I like hotdogs just fine, but I never had a guy take me out for hotdogs on a first date," I say.

"Trust me, these are the finest dogs in town," he says. He lifts his head in a nod toward the guy standing behind the cart. "Hey Alex, what's up?"

The man nods back and reaches his hand out to Judd. They give each other a sort of slap, high-five, hand-shake combo. "What's up, my man? Who's this gorgeous lady?"

"This is Bailey," he says. "Bailey, this is Alex."

I take my hand out of Judd's so I can shake hands with the cart owner. "Nice to meet you," I say.

He takes my hand in his and gives it a soft kiss. "My pleasure," he says, his Spanish accent thick. "What can I get for you, my dear."

"I'll take a hot dog with mustard and relish," I say. "I don't think I've had a hotdog since I was a kid."

"You're kidding," Judd says. "Hotdogs are a college staple."

"Says you," I tease. "And you're a med-student? I thought you'd be eating nothing but health foods. No offense, Alex."

"None taken," Alex says with a laugh as he fixes my hotdog and hands it over to me.

He doesn't ask for Judd's order. He just pulls out two hotdogs and loads them up with chili, onions, ketchup, mustard and pickles.

Judd hands him a wad of ones and thanks him. We walk over to a wooden bench that faces out toward the shore and sit down.

"Do you know everyone around here?" I ask. He seems to relate to people easily. Something about that smile makes him very approachable and easy to like.

"Not everyone," he says. "I just like my routines I guess."

I take a bite of my hotdog and a dollop of mustard slides out the back and onto my jeans. I stare at it, not believing I just did that. I close my eyes and feel like giving up.

Judd laughs and pours water on his napkin, then cleans up the blob on my leg.

"I've never been so accident-prone in my life," I say. "I swear to god."

He smiles. "I believe you," he says. "I think it's kind of cute, though."

"This," I point toward my mismatched, stained outfit, "is not cute."

In response, he just lets his eyes roam over my body. Nervous energy buzzes through me.

"I think you could wear just about anything and look good," he says.

Warmth spreads up my cheeks. I continue eating my hotdog, but scoot just a tiny bit closer to him on the bench.

"So, hotdogs," I say, laughing. "Is this a nightly ritual for you?"

"A couple times a week. Hotdogs might not be healthy, but they're fast and cheap," Judd says. "I'm on scholarship here and it's awesome, but I don't get much of a stipend and I don't have time to get a job. I've got a special project going on right now and it's taking up a lot of time."

Disappointment shoots through me. If he doesn't have enough time for a job, he's definitely not going to have time to have a girlfriend. But then I stop myself. This is exactly what I always did with Preston. I was always getting way ahead of myself when it came to our future. I actually thought he was close to proposing to me, and instead he was ready to completely cast me aside.

Judd kisses me once and takes me on a hotdog date and suddenly I'm ready to be his girlfriend. I'm so lame.

"I never asked you where you're from," I say, trying to keep conversation moving so I can stop daydreaming.

"A small town west of here," he says. "Cochran. Have you heard of it?"

"I think so," I say. "Is that near Macon?"

"Not really," he says. "Maybe forty-five minutes drive from there."

"What brought you to Fairhope?" I ask. "The scholarship?"

"Yes," he says. "I went to UGA for undergrad, graduated with honors and applied to a bunch of med schools all over the South. Fairhope offered me the best deal. Plus, it's on the beach. That doesn't hurt."

I smile.

"What about you?" he asks. He's already devoured one of the hotdogs and is starting on the second. "Where are you from?"

"You're looking at it," I say.

"You're a townie?"

I scrunch my nose. "You make it sound so dirty," I say. "And yes, Fairhope born and raised."

"That makes sense," he says, nodding. He makes a strange face.

"What is that supposed to mean?"

He clears his throat. "It didn't entirely escape my notice that you've been dating Preston Wright for a long time," he says.

I draw in a tense breath. I guess the subject of Preston was bound to come up eventually, but I wasn't expecting Judd to bring it up tonight. Still, there's a part of me that's surprised he'd noticed me enough before yesterday to know who I was dating.

"I'm pretty sure discussing ex-boyfriends on a first date is listed in the rule book on the don't side," I say.

He laughs. "I'm not really one for following the rules," he says. "I'd rather just get it all out in the open, anyway. I want to get to know you, and it's obvious he's been a big part of your life. There's no reason to dance around it."

I'm surprised by his honesty and the fact that he doesn't mind talking about something like this so early.

Still, my heartbreak is so fresh, I'm afraid he'll hear it in my voice. And I don't want to ruin tonight the way I did last night. It's rare to get a second chance at any relationship. A third would be way too much to ask.

"You don't have to talk about it if you don't want to," he says.

"It's okay," I say. I take a deep breath, not really sure what to say. "Preston and I got together senior year in high school. He'd been dating one of my best friends and she left to go to school up north."

I don't mention the fact that they were still together when I started sleeping with him behind Leigh Anne's back. Being the other girl and betraying one of my friends like that is one of the most shameful things of my life. I definitely don't want Judd to know that about me. Ever.

"Ouch," he says. "That had to be complicated."

"To say the least," I say. "She's recently come back to town and it's been tough. The truth is, I don't think he ever really got over her, you know? I was always second best, in a way."

"That's not possible," Judd says. "You deserve more than that."

Guilt twists my heart. "You don't know that," I say. "I've done some bad things. Things I'm not proud of."

"We all have," he says. "That doesn't mean you don't deserve to be someone's first choice."

I look over at him. The only light out here is a distant lamp and the light of a nearly full moon. If he knew the truth of how Preston and I got together, he wouldn't be saying that.

"Preston never really told me he was still in love with her, but I think I always knew," I say. "And when she got back, things changed between us."

"Did they get back together or something?" he asks, his voice gentle.

"No, she fell for someone else, but Preston grew more and more distant over the summer. Then this fall his twin sister, Penny, took off for a few months with his best friend. When she came back, we all found out she was pregnant. She almost lost the baby and was on bed rest for a few weeks. Preston was really great to her. He barely left her side. We didn't see each other much."

I shrug, feeling the sting of fresh tears. I push them back, so tired of always being one step away from a complete breakdown. Talking about this with someone new is hard, but the fact that it's a guy I'm interested in just makes it harder.

"He broke things off?"

I nod. "About three weeks ago," I say. "I guess I saw it coming, but I think I was in denial for a while. When he finally said the words, it was devastating."

Judd rests his hand on top of mine. "I'm sorry."

I sniff, doing everything I can to hold back the tears. He's already seen me cry twice. I can't let this be a third. If there really is a first-date rule book, I'm certain crying about breaking up with your ex is at the very top of the 'don't' page in bright red capital letters.

"I can't believe I'm telling you all this," I say.

"I didn't mean to make you upset," he says. "I just wanted you to know it's okay to talk about it with me. In my experience, it's better to get this kind of stuff out in the open right from the start. No secrets. No surprises."

"Does that mean you're going to tell me about your ex-girlfriends now?" I ask. "Because I'm really looking forward to that."

He laughs. "Are you being sarcastic?"

"No," I say in a big voice. "I love to hear about ex-girlfriends on a first date. Especially your sex life, don't leave those details out."

He squeezes my hand. "I'm afraid my story isn't very interesting anyway," he says, laughing. "I was a geek in high school and didn't really date anyone until I got to college. I dated a few girls here and there, then I met Mandy. We dated for about a year. I fell head over heels in love with her, thought we were going to get married and have babies together."

His confession takes my breath away. Guys don't really admit this kind of stuff very often. "What happened?"

"Oh, we're still together," he says, casually. "She's at home with our three kids."

He says it so deadpan, I almost think he's serious. Then, he breaks out in that sly smile of his and I smack him hard on the shoulder.

"You asshole," I scream. "I thought you were serious."

He holds his shoulder and leans away from me, laughing so hard it echoes across the darkness.

"I'm sorry, but the look on your face was priceless," he says.

"I could kill you for that," I say.

He stands and tosses his trash into the metal can beside the row of benches. "Things were getting way too serious," he says. "I had to lighten the mood."

"By making me think you were here with me while your

wife sits at home with the babies?" I ask. "You have a twisted mind."

"Seriously," he says. "I'm sweet."

"Sweet and apparently twisted." I roll my eyes and pretend to be upset, but I can't keep up the act for long. He's too adorable.

"What really happened?" I ask.

He takes my hand again and we start walking down the boardwalk toward the pier.

"She dumped me," he says. "For her ex-boyfriend. It devastated me at the time, but then I came here and slowly, day-by-day, it stopped hurting so much."

I swallow, thinking about Preston and how I've spent the last few weeks barely able to get out of bed every morning.

Knowing he's been there makes this better somehow.

We walk together for a while without saying anything. The waves crash against the shore just steps away from us, the high tide at its peak. A cold breeze whips past us, and I lean into him as we walk, letting his body be my shield.

"Do you want to walk up on the pier?" he asks.

"Sure," I say.

He leads me up onto the wooden pier. It's only about seven-thirty and the fishermen are taking advantage of the changing tides. They hang their sturdy poles over the side, many of them baiting hooks and casting out into the dark abyss beyond.

Lights like lamp-posts are situated every ten feet or so, illuminating the worn boards along the length of the pier.

We walk all the way down to the very end and find an empty spot along the railing to stand and stare out at the water. Because of the lights, we can just make out the water below. From here, it looks dark navy in color, peaks of white frothing up here and there and catching the light.

I place my feet on the first rail and lean over the edge to look straight down and a rush of fear goes through me. I welcome it, loving that feeling when my stomach seems to drop out from under me like I'm on a rollercoaster.

Judd puts his hands around my waist, as if holding onto me for dear life.

I laugh and step back down to his level. "Scared?"

"You were freaking me out," he says. "Don't lean so far over. What if you fell?"

I lean one arm all the way over the side and raise my eyebrows at him. "What about this? Is this scary?"

He pretends to hide his eyes. "I'm serious, don't do that."

I throw my arms around him. "I'm sorry," I say. "Are you scared of heights or something?"

"No," he says. "I'm just scared of really deep, possibly shark-infested waters. Especially when it's dark outside. Haven't you ever seen Jaws?"

I sigh. "There aren't any great white sharks off the coast here," I say.

"How do you know?" he asks. He leans cautiously over the side and looks down. "There could be anything under the curtain of that darkness."

I put my hands on the wooden railing and lift my chin as the wind blows across my cheeks. My ears are freezing, so I lift my hands up to my bun and let my hair down.

Inside the center of the bun, my hair is still a little bit wet. I run my hands through it and shake my head, letting it fall heavy down my back.

The wind whips it across my face, and I close my eyes.

"This is one of my favorite feelings in the whole world," I say, breathing in the crisp smell of salt water.

Judd steps closer, warmth radiating from his body. Something in the air between us shifts. He runs a hand through my hair, pushing it behind my ear and placing his palm against my face.

I open my eyes, my heart racing uncontrollably.

When I turn to face him, I recognize the desire in his eyes.

Only tonight, there's no alcohol to fuel it. It's pure and real and undeniably hot.

I lean into his hand, my flesh burning under his touch. His fingers twitch slightly, as if he wants to pull me closer.

I want to kiss him, but I'm scared. I don't want to be rejected again. I don't want to misunderstand. And I don't want to fall too fast just because I'm so hungry for something to heal my broken heart.

But I'm helpless to stop it.

When he leans down, he stops short, waiting for me to make a decision. I lift my head ever so slightly and he closes the space between us, his fingers tangling in the hair at the nape of my neck. He takes my mouth more forcefully than he did last night, and my body lights up at the first meeting of our lips.

Our lips open and explore. Our tongues dance and our bodies press together.

My hands slip around his waist. I'm so aware of the fabric at the edge of his shirt, wanting nothing more than to slide my hand under and up. To feel the warm skin underneath and the hard muscles I know I'll find along his back.

I want it so badly, I almost can't control the desire.

He releases my lips and moves his kisses along the line of my chin. When he gets closer to my ear, he whispers, "You're so beautiful."

I immediately want to tell him he's wrong. That he must not see me for some reason. But I hold it in, letting myself hear him. Not quite believing, but for the first time in a long time, wanting to believe.

CHAPTER 12

Judd and I spend the rest of the evening walking along the beach, popping into shops along the boardwalk before we finally give in to the cold and head back to his car.

He rolls down the windows of his car and turns on the local radio station, which is playing nonstop Christmas music for the entire month of December. He pops the trunk of his beat-up Toyota and pulls out a large blue blanket.

I laugh. "So not only do you always come prepared with bandages for when you accidentally injure a girl, you also carry a king-size blanket in your trunk for romantic moments."

His eyes widen. "I can put it back in the trunk if you're going to make fun of it," he says, looking so serious. "Big blue has been with me for a long time."

"Big blue?" I ask, realizing my stomach muscles hurt from laughing so much. "Please tell me you didn't actually name your blanket."

"Oh yes I did," he says. He slams the trunk closed and motions for me to sit down on the hood of the car. I climb up and he wraps the blanket around my shoulders. "I've had this blanket since I was a kid. We've had some good times."

"I bet," I say.

"When my brother and I were little, my mom bought us matching blankets. His was red, mine was blue." He climbs up beside me and we snuggled close under the blanket. "We used to use them to build tents in the living room. Mom would let us leave them up for days and we'd sleep under there and hang out talking all night long. Those were the days."

I smile. "I didn't know you had a brother."

He nods. "Jonathan. He was two years older than me." There's a sadness in his voice and when I turn to look at him, I see that his eyes are shining.

Then I realize he used the word 'was'.

My heart tightens in my chest. "What happened?" I ask, my voice almost a whisper.

He takes a long breath in, then shakes his head. "I never talk about this," he says. He looks at me and as our eyes meet, I can't help but feel there's something real here between us. "He died four years ago. Acute myeloid leukemia. By the time the doctors gave an official diagnosis, the disease was too far advanced. He needed a bone marrow transplant to survive and they couldn't find a donor in time."

I reach for his hand under the blanket. "I'm so sorry," I say. I know the words aren't enough for what he's been through, but I don't know what else to say.

"His disease is what made me want to be a doctor," he says. "If there was some way I could help, even just a little bit, so that someone else doesn't have to go through that with someone they love..."

His voice trails off and we sit together in silence, the only sound the beating of the waves on the nearby shore. I lay my head against his shoulder and he wraps his arm around my waist, pulling me closer.

Finally, he straightens and I sit up.

"I didn't mean to totally ruin the mood of the date," he says with a laugh.

"You didn't."

"A little," he says. "I don't even know why I told you about Jonathan. Especially on our first date. For some reason, I just feel like I can be myself around you. Like no matter what I say, you aren't going to judge me or hurt me."

A shiver goes through my body despite the heat we've created under the blanket. "I feel the same way," I say.

And I do. I've spent so many years trying to be the person I thought Preston and our friends wanted me to be that I never really felt comfortable just being myself. It's strange and different and wonderfully freeing.

Our eyes meet in the half-darkness and my heart begins to beat faster. His grasp around my waist tightens and he pulls me closer, his fingers digging into my hip. I turn my body slightly toward him, our legs pressed firmly against each other.

Judd leans down, his lips finding mine in one breathless moment. And this kiss is different. It isn't just a kiss of discovery or new attraction. This kiss is deeper, less tentative. As if we're sure of each other now, knowing this is more than something physical. Knowing we can trust each other in ways we weren't expecting.

When we part, I hide my head against his chest. There's something stirring deep within me I wasn't expecting. Something I never could have hoped for after losing Preston. Something I never knew I could feel.

"When can I see you again?" Judd asks. His voice is husky and deep, full of desire.

Is tomorrow too soon? I've never really done this before. With Preston, the beginning was a game of hide and seek. Stolen moments. I've never dated someone like Judd before. I don't want to scare him off, but I guess if nothing's scared him off yet, telling him I want to see him as soon as possible shouldn't be too bad either.

"Is it wrong to say I want to see you tomorrow?" I ask.

He smiles and it sends an electric jolt through my insides. "Not at all," he says. "I was really hoping you'd say that."

"The only problem is that I've gotten really behind on school lately," I say. "If I don't nail my finals, I'm going to be in some serious trouble in a few of my classes. I've got to spend all next week studying as much as possible before finals start."

"We can study together," he says.

I turn my head to the side and cut my eyes toward him. "You're too distracting," I say. "We won't get anything done."

He laughs. "I swear," he says. "We'll just study and I promise not to distract you too much. Unless we're taking a break."

I think about it for a second. It's definitely tempting. I want to spend more time with him before Christmas break. I don't even know if he's going home for the break or sticking around, but I don't want to miss out on seeing him just so I can study.

"Okay," I say. "We'll try it for one night and see how it goes."

"Tomorrow night?"

"I get off work at four," I say.

"Perfect," he says. "I'll come by the cafe and pick you up. We can head back to my place if you want."

"I want," I say.

Judd pulls me into another kiss, and for the first time since Preston and I broke up, I'm looking forward to tomorrow.

CHAPTER 13

I'm practically floating when I walk into my apartment late that evening.

Monica is lying on the couch in her pj's watching TV and eating popcorn. She has all the lights off except the strings of Christmas lights we've tacked to the walls.

She eyes me curiously. "What in the world happened to you?" she asks. She grabs the remote and mutes the television. "You look like the cat who ate the canary."

I cannot control the huge smile that spreads across my face. I lean against the front door and sigh. "Nothing. Just the most magical, surprising night of my life."

Her eyes nearly pop out of her head. She clears a spot for me beside her on the couch and pats her hand on the cushions. "Spill it," she demands.

I move to sit beside her and am not surprised to see she's watching old episodes of Firefly. Again. She's obsessed with that show.

"Judd came in to The Cup today," I say.

She bounces beside me and when I look over, her lips are pressed together so tight, they're turning white.

"At first, it was a complete disaster," I say. "I spilled coffee all over myself and had to change into the boss's over-sized t-shirt. I kept tripping over chairs and knocking things over every time I saw him glance my way. I thought for sure this guy must think I'm a lunatic. I expected him to leave any second and never come back."

Monica turns her body all the way toward me. She's shoving popcorn in her mouth like I'm the best entertainment she's had in weeks. "And?"

"And he never left," I say. I know I'm blushing because my entire face is red hot. I can't stop smiling. "He stayed until we were the only two left in the cafe, and when we finally started talking, he asked me out."

"Ahhh!" Monica nearly spills her popcorn as she throws her arms around my neck. "This is awesome. When are you guys going out?"

"We already did. Sort of," I say. I tell her all about our hotdogs and our walk to the pier. I leave out the bit about his brother, because he seemed kind of protective about that information, but I tell her everything else.

"I knew something like this would happen," she says. "You just needed to get out of the house and put yourself back on the market."

"I'm not a house," I say. "It's not like I was looking for someone new."

"That's what they say, though, isn't it? Love comes along when you least expect it."

I roll my eyes. "This isn't love, Mon. We just met."

Still, there's a tingle that goes through me from head to toe just thinking about Judd and the possibility of a future with someone new. It might not be love, but it's definitely like.

"That's how it starts for everyone, though," she says. "When are you going to see him again? Did you guys talk about it?"

"Tomorrow," I say, smiling again. "We're going to have a study date."

She laughs. "Right. A study date."

I push her with my elbow. "We're really going to study," I say in my own defense. "If I fail my exams, I'm going to be on probation. I really can't afford that."

"Well, I'm very happy for you," she says. "This is exactly what the doctor ordered. If you had spent one more day moping around this apartment, I was going to have to move out or kick you out, one or the other."

I scrunch my nose. "Was it really that bad?"

"Worse," she says. "But it's really good to see you smiling again."

I grab a handful of her popcorn and she turns the sound back on. While we watch TV, I think about how good it feels to be smiling again and how quickly Judd was able to turn me from depression to happiness.

At the same time, though, I can't help but wonder if I'm making a big mistake getting involved with someone new. What if he breaks my heart just like Preston did? Would I be able to survive another bad breakup so soon?

I know I'm getting way ahead of myself. One date doesn't

make him my boyfriend, but I already feel like I'm falling for him. It's all happening way too fast, and I'm terrified if I go any deeper, I'll just be opening myself up to a pain my heart can't handle.

CHAPTER 14

Work seems to drag by the next day. Every single time the bell over the door rings, my heart leaps and I look up hoping to see Judd walk through.

And every time it isn't him, my heart sinks back down into my chest.

I'm scared of how much I want to see him. Is this normal for a new relationship? Can I even call what we have so far a relationship? I have no idea what I'm doing or how this is supposed to go, and I feel like a lost puppy.

We haven't even talked about what we're looking for right now. Maybe he isn't interested in a relationship. I know medical school can be extremely tough and he said he has to work extra hours for his scholarship project. Does he even have time for a real girlfriend or is this just a fling?

Of course, if it was a fling, he would have slept with me that first night in the bar instead of trying to slow things down.

These are the neurotic thoughts occupying my mind throughout my shift. The closer it gets to my four o'clock shift end, the more neurotic and paranoid I become.

What if he isn't even coming? I don't have his phone number or anything, so it would be easy for him to ditch me if he wanted to.

By ten minutes to four, I've completely convinced myself he isn't coming and that he doesn't want to see me again. I must have done something last night to mess this whole thing up. And maybe he's really not as good looking and sweet as I thought he was and he's doing me a favor by blowing me off. That's when the bell sounds and he finally walks in.

I'm cleaning off a table in the far corner when he casually walks up to the counter and orders a caramel mocha. His eyes drift toward me and he winks.

I almost pass out in a mix of relief and desire. Yeah, he's definitely every bit as good looking as I remember. He's wearing a pair of dark blue jeans and a long-sleeve cotton t-shirt that shows off the defined muscles underneath. His hair is slightly wavier than I've seen it before, and I wonder if that's because of the misty rain outside today. Whatever it is, I like it.

"Hey," he says, walking over to the table where I'm cleaning.

"Hi," I say back, feeling like a teenager with a new crush.

"Are we still on for four?"

Fuck yes.

"Yeah, I just need a few minutes to cash out and clean up in the back," I say. "I'll be out in a few minutes."

He nods and takes a seat in an empty booth. He doesn't

have his backpack with him today, but he pulls a book out of his back pocket and opens it to a page marked with a tattered scrap of paper.

I stare at the book cover as I make my way back to the kitchen. King. He's reading Stephen King, my all-time favorite author. I nearly swoon as I turn the corner and disappear into the back room.

He's ruggedly handsome, loves The Beatles, reads books in his spare time, and still carries a sentimental blanket from his childhood in his car. He's too perfect.

Which means there has to be a catch, right? If something (or someone) seems too good to be true, it probably is. Or at least that's what my mother has always told me. There has to be something wrong with him.

I warn my heart to be careful. To hold back and put up walls to protect myself.

But deep inside, I already know I'm in too deep. Just a few days with this guy and already I care about him more than I should. Whatever outer shell I had been keeping up around my heart, it broke that night while I was dancing. And when Judd appeared out of nowhere like a gift from the universe, he slipped inside to the place where I am most vulnerable.

It's way too late for being careful.

CHAPTER 15

When we pull up to Judd's apartment, I'm surprised to find he lives in the same complex as Preston. I can't help but take a quick look around for Preston's car. He always parks in the same spot just in front of his building, but the spot is empty and I breathe a sigh of relief.

I don't feel like facing him today.

In the three weeks since we broke up, I've only run into Preston a handful of times, and every time I feel like the victim of a drive-by shooting.

The first time was by far the worst. I had been crying for three days straight and was rushing to class. My hair was in a messy, knotted ponytail and I hadn't had time to put on any makeup. Not even lipgloss. I was wearing a pair of yoga pants with a hole in the knee and a baggy sweatshirt. Normally I wouldn't be caught dead looking like that in public, but I'd missed so many classes I knew I couldn't afford to miss another. I woke up late and had no choice but to run out looking like a homeless person.

So of course that was the day I ran into Preston. He looked gorgeous and happy and completely unaffected by our breakup.

I wanted to crawl under a rock and hide, but by the time I saw him, it was too late. He'd already seen me and was making his way over to talk to me.

I'll never forget the look of pity in his eyes or the way he casually touched my elbow and asked if I was doing okay. I lied and said I was doing fine, but there was no way he believed me.

I vowed then and there to a) avoid him at all costs until I could pull myself together and b) to always leave the house looking pristine and gorgeous, just in case.

Still, even when I look perfect, nothing has been able to mask the sadness in my eyes.

It's gotten better with time, but the sadness returns every time he talks to me. I don't want Judd to see that. I also don't really know how I feel about Preston seeing me with another guy. No matter how much I like Judd, Preston was my heart for years and I don't want to see him until I know I can look at him without feeling sad and broken.

"Everything okay?" Judd asks as he pushes the door to his apartment open. He follows my gaze toward the parking lot and a hint of sadness crosses his features.

Crap. He knows. Of course he knows. If he's been living here, he surely knows who parks in that spot.

"Yes, I'm fine," I say, pushing past the awkward feeling in my stomach as I walk into his apartment.

It's definitely a bachelor's apartment, but not as bad as it could be. The furnishings are sparse and there aren't any pictures or anything on the white walls, but at least it's not messy like most guys' places. The only Christmas decoration is a sad looking little tree on the kitchen counter.

"Welcome to my humble abode," he says. "It's not much, but it's part of my scholarship, so it's home for at least a few more years."

"It's great," I say. "Much nicer than my apartment."

Even with a roommate and a part-time job, I couldn't afford to live on this side of town. The rent here is more than $1200 a month. I know because I really wanted to live closer to Preston and looked into it when he first got his own place.

"I don't know about that," he says. "I don't have much furniture here, but it's comfortable and I like having the space."

"Do you live here alone?" From the looks of it, it's a two-bedroom apartment, but I don't see any signs of a roommate.

"Yep," he says. "I set up an office in the second bedroom, but I hardly ever use it. I prefer The Cup. Better view."

He smiles at me and I'm blushing again. How he can think I look good in my work uniform is beyond me. And just how long has he been noticing me?

"Do you mind if I use your bathroom?" I ask.

Unlike yesterday, today I came prepared. I brought a change of clothes so I wouldn't be stuck in my t-shirt and black pants. Besides, when I get off work, I always stink of coffee.

Without taking a shower, there's not much I can do about the coffee smell since it's in my hair and pretty much soaked into my pores, but at the very least I can change my clothes and put on some fresh makeup.

"No problem," he says. "Do you want some hot chocolate or something?"

"Anything but coffee," I say as I disappear into the bathroom with my bag.

I move as quickly as I can, pulling my hair out of its long braid and brushing it. The braid has given it a bit of a pretty wave, so I decide to just put a quick clip in it to hold it out of my eyes, but leave it mostly down.

I freshen my makeup and quickly change into a pair of jeans and a sweater that hugs my curves in all the right ways.

I brush my teeth, stuff my dirty clothes deep into my bag and head back out into the living room.

Judd is sitting at the small table in his living room. There are two steaming cups of hot chocolate sitting out and he has his books spread in front of him. He's leaning over one of the books, a highlighter in his hand, his hair falling across his face.

He's so different from Preston and watching him now, it occurs to me all over again. Preston never wanted to study together. He said he preferred to study alone because I talked too much.

Watching Judd now, I wonder how long it will take before I stop comparing him to Preston.

So far, he seems to be a better match for me than Preston. I feel like I can be myself around Judd without all the pressure of trying so hard to make him happy. He's just happy to simply be around me and that thought creates a beautiful new hope in my heart.

Maybe Monica was right. Maybe there really is someone out there for me.

Maybe he's been right here in front of me this whole time.

CHAPTER 16

J udd looks up and smiles.

"Wow, you look great," he says, standing. His eyes travel down the length of my body.

He pushes his long dark-blond hair behind his ear and pulls out the empty chair across from him. "I made some hot chocolate, but there's bottled water and soda in the fridge if you want something else."

He's so nice to me, I can hardly stand it. I'm not used to this kind of attention at all. Not that Preston was a bad guy or anything, but he never really treated me like this. Most of Preston's gestures came from extravagant gifts and flowers, particularly when he'd done something to upset me. Judd just seems to be a super nice guy all the time. It's almost difficult to trust it. Like I'm waiting for him to suddenly turn all Mr. Hyde on me and start screaming at me for something stupid and irrational.

I sit down and rummage through my backpack for the

books I brought, then lay them out on the table along with my laptop.

"What's first?" he asks, then leans over the back of my chair. His hair falls down across my cheek and I inhale the scent of his shampoo. He smells woodsy and fresh, like he just showered moments before he picked me up.

I shiver from his closeness, knowing that all I'd have to do is turn my head and our lips would almost touch.

I clear my throat and try to concentrate on the material in front of me. Good guy or not, he's hot and there's something about him that makes my body tingle.

"Um, statistics?" It comes out as more of a question than an answer. Why do I always feel so nervous and mixed up around him? I'm either running into doors or knocking shit over. It's a miracle he's even interested in me at all. "You?"

"Fundamentals of Immunology," he says.

I raise my eyebrows and suck in a breath. This guy is light-years ahead of me in the smarts department. Surely I can't really be the kind of girl he's looking for.

"What year med student are you, anyway?"

"First year," he says. "I haven't really been in Fairhope very long."

That would make him probably around twenty-two or twenty-three years old, I'm guessing. Still, he seems so much more mature than most of the guys I know. Maybe that comes partially from losing his brother.

"You're a junior, right?" he asks. He moves back around the table to sit down across from me.

I relax slightly now that he's not hovering over me with his lips practically within kissing distance.

"Yeah," I say. "And I'll still be one this time next year if I don't start studying. I'm honestly not exaggerating when I say I'm on the cusp of failing half my courses this semester."

I don't elaborate on the fact that it's more from my lack of going to class than it is my lack of understanding the subject matter.

"Okay, I get it," he says with a sly smile. "We better get to work. Would you rather listen to music or have it quiet in here?"

I almost always study with my headphones in and my iPhone blasting music. "I like music, but if you like it quiet, I can just put my headphones in," I say.

"I like music, too," he says. "I'll just turn on one of my play-lists and you can let me know if you want to hear something else."

I nod and pretend not to stare as he fiddles with the stereo behind him. Still, he's bent over and wearing a pair of very sexy jeans that show off his muscular legs and ass. How can I be expected to do anything but stare and drool?

I'm beginning to wonder if this studying together thing was really such a great idea. As much as I want to spend time with him, I really do need to pass these finals with flying colors. My parents will kill me if I flunk any classes and have to retake them. They aren't poor or anything, but it's not like they have a bunch of money lying around, either. They agreed to pay for my tuition as long as I keep my grades up, but if I fail I don't know what they'll do.

They know how upset I've been over this breakup, but I'm not sure it will be enough to excuse a whole semester down the drain.

There's no way I'll be able to pay my own tuition with the little bit I make at The Cup. I can barely pay the rent most months as it is. I have no choice but to buckle down so I can ace my finals.

Judd gets the music started and I'm surprised to hear he's chosen Classical music instead of rock.

"Mozart," he says. "It's good for your brain and for remembering things. At least that's what I've read."

I shrug and decide to give it a shot. I could use all the help I can get right now.

We settle into a happy silence as we both dive into our books, but after a few minutes, his foot brushes mine under the table. When I look up to see if he did it on purpose, he smiles.

CHAPTER 17

It's dead week on campus and for the next few days, Judd and I spend every chance we get together. We study, walk on the beach, eat more than our fair share of hotdogs, and spend a couple of nights snuggled under Big Blue, watching the waves crash on the shore.

I gradually fill his apartment with little Christmas baubles. My own apartment is always overflowing anyway.

"You must really love Christmas," he says when I walk through the door with yet another strand of lights and a plastic snowman.

"Doesn't everyone?" I ask.

He doesn't answer. He simply smiles and watches as I hang the lights. "If you could have one Christmas wish this year, what would be?" he asks.

I bite my lip and look up toward the ceiling. That's a tough one.

"I wish it would snow," I say.

He raises an eyebrow and I shrug.

"I know it's impossible," I say. "But I've always dreamed about snow on Christmas. There's just something magical about it, don't you think? Only, it never snows in Fairhope. Ever."

"Maybe this year," he says, pulling me into his arms. "This is a magical year."

We've been doing a good job studying when we have to, but our evenings usually end up with us finally giving in to our desires and making out on the couch. It's getting more and more difficult to be careful with my heart.

When I'm working, he always stops by to study, and I'm getting spoiled by all the attention.

With Preston, I always felt like I was begging for his attention. When I wanted to hang out, it was always me calling him first or asking what he wanted to do. If he had a big family function, it was always me asking if I could come. Even with the Christmas Memories Charity Ball, I was the one who had officially asked him if he wanted to go with me or not. I learned the hard way that unless I nailed things down early, Preston would never make plans to spend time with me.

Every once in a while, as much as I hate it, thoughts of Preston invade my brain. Most of the time, it's as if my brain and my heart want to make simple comparisons between the two guys. If Judd opens the door for me, I think about how Preston always did that too. If Judd tells me I look beautiful when I'm wearing something simple like yoga pants and a tank top, I think about the fact that Preston never commented on how I looked unless I was dressed up for a special occasion.

I know it's not exactly a competition, but in most areas of comparison, Judd is winning by a mile.

He's sweet and thoughtful. He always compliments me and pays attention to me. He asks me for my opinion and seems to really care what my answer is.

So why am I even still thinking of Preston at all?

"It's like wearing in a new pair of shoes," Monica says the following Sunday afternoon when I bring it up. She's sitting on the couch and I'm in the kitchen making grilled cheese for lunch. "If you adored your old shoes and they were super comfortable after a few years of wearing them, it's only natural to be hesitant to really believe the new shoes could ever be as good. You kind of have to wear them in a bit. Get comfortable with how nice and shiny and new they are. When you finally start to appreciate the new shoes for how great they are, that's when you start to see the flaws in the old ones. The holes. The scuffs. All the problems."

"The shoe analogy isn't really doing it for me," I say.

She rolls her eyes. "I'm just saying it's only natural for you to compare them. I mean, you loved Preston, right?"

I shrug.

This is something else I've been giving a lot of thought to these days. Did I really ever love Preston? Or did I love the idea of him?

When we first got together in high school, capturing his attention was more like a game. I was immature and jealous of everything Leigh Anne did. I wasn't out to hurt her. Not intentionally, anyway. But I wanted him because he was the cutest, richest guy in school. He was the one everyone wanted. So I wanted him, too.

And at first, it was just sex. Pure fun. I think we both got kind of high off the idea of sneaking around behind everyone's backs. It was fun to have this secret between us.

Then Leigh Anne walked in on us in the pool-house one day and all the fun died. Preston wanted nothing to do with me for a long time. He tried everything he could think of to get Leigh Anne back, but once she decided to move to Boston for school, he knew he'd lost her forever.

Gradually, he came back to me. Over time, especially when she didn't come home for the holidays—or for anything—he moved on and we got comfortable. It took him almost a year before he ever called me his girlfriend, though. To be honest, I don't think he ever really thought of me as his girl. I was more like a layover until he found something better. Never worthy of what he had to offer. Never quite good enough.

Or at least that was my fear.

"Are you saying you didn't love him?" Monica asks. She's off the couch now and standing in the doorway of our small kitchen, her arms crossed in front of her chest.

"I don't really know anymore," I say. "Maybe I was just obsessed with this perfect idea of getting married to the guy everyone else wanted."

"Wow," she says, her jaw hanging open. "This is a huge realization. Do you even realize how huge this is?"

I shrug again. I'm not even sure I really want to be talking about this. In some ways, I'm completely freaked out about this whole thing. If I can admit that I never really loved Preston, that means I'm well on my way to getting over him completely.

Which means I'm open to falling in love with someone else.

And the idea of falling for someone as perfect as Judd scares the ever-loving shit out of me.

"Bailey, listen to me," she says. She walks over and grabs my arm, turning me toward her so I am forced to look in her eyes. "For as long as I've known you, you've had your head so far up Preston's ass that you could barely remember your name."

I frown. I wasn't that bad.

Was I?

"You never made plans for the weekend without checking with him first. You never left this house without looking perfectly put-together and color-coordinated," she says, ticking off her reasons on her fingers. "Preston never once came over to our place to hang out, and he certainly never just stopped by to see you on a whim. If you wanted to be with him, you were always having to go to him."

"I liked the shoe analogy better," I murmur, turning back to take the sandwich off the skillet before it burns.

"When he dumped you, you stayed in bed for days. Weeks. You slept all day, remember? Missed classes?"

"What exactly are you getting at here?" I ask.

"I'm saying that a few weeks ago if I had told you that Preston was the wrong guy for you, you would have possibly injured my face," she says. "But now that you have someone like Judd to compare him to, you're finally starting to see that despite his good looks and reputation and money and all that, Preston really wasn't the one. This. Is. Huge."

My hand trembles as I reach to turn off the burner. My stomach feels hollow and my nerves feel jittery.

She's right. I know she's right.

And the truth scares me to death. Because if I didn't even

really love Preston and it still hurt that fucking bad when he rejected me, what is it going to feel like when someone I truly fall for says he doesn't want me anymore?

I don't know that I'll be able to survive it.

The thought of that kind of pain makes me want to run screaming in the opposite direction the next time Judd Kohler comes knocking at my door.

"What's going on in your beautiful brain?" she asks. Monica takes our plates to the table while I make drinks and grab the napkins.

By the time I sit down across from her, I'm no closer to a coherent answer.

"Is it crazy that I don't want to see Judd again, because I'm scared of what will happen if he breaks my heart?" I ask. "I mean, it's messed up right? That I'd give up the chance at something real just because I don't want to get hurt?"

She reaches across the table and squeezes my hand. "I'm pretty sure it's normal," she says. Then she smiles and raises one eyebrow. "Besides. I can tell from the way you blush and smile every time he's around that you're in too deep to turn away now, anyway. If he called right now, you'd hop in the car and go meet him in a heartbeat. Broken heart be damned."

I laugh and take a bite of my grilled cheese.

I hate to admit it, but she's right. It's crazy how quickly it can happen. In just one short week, I went from barely able to get out of bed to a racing heart every time the phone rings.

About two seconds later, that's exactly what happens. I jump at the sound, then race toward where I left my phone sitting on the counter. I take one look at the caller ID and my face breaks out in a huge smile.

Monica laughs. "Told ya."

CHAPTER 18

I stick my tongue out at my roommate, then pick up the phone and walk back toward my bedroom.

"Hey," I say, a warm feeling spreading through my body.

"Hey, what are you up to tonight?" he asks.

We hadn't made any specific plans to be together tonight , but I had been hoping he would call.

"Nothing in particular," I say. "You?"

"Can you be ready around six?" he asks.

"Ready for what?" I ask. My stomach flips. What exactly does he have in mind?

"I want to take you out to meet some of my friends," he says, like it's the most casual thing in the universe.

My entire body tenses. I wasn't expecting to meet his friends so soon. I have no idea what to wear or how to act around them.

"What were you guys planning to do?" I ask, trying not to sound like I'm about to throw up.

"We were going to head to my buddy Brian's house and play some games," he says. "He's having a little get-together for Christmas. It's pretty casual, but I'd like to go."

I hesitate. Breathe in and out. I'm not sure I'm ready for this. Meeting the friends is a huge deal. What if they don't like me? What if I don't fit in with them? It took me years to learn how to fit in with the rich kids at Fairhope High. Even up until the point Preston and I broke up, I never really felt like I could be one-hundred-percent myself around them. And since we broke up? Not one of my so-called friends has bothered to come by and check on me or ask me to hang out.

It didn't take long for me to see the true loyalties there.

I was never one of them, and maybe that was part of the reason Preston and I never really fit.

"I don't know," I say. "It seems like a big step."

"Wait, are you saying no?" he asks. He sounds surprised. Worried. "Look, it's not a big deal if you really don't want to come, but it's not like I'm asking you to marry me or anything. It's just a party."

He says it with a laugh, but for some reason, his words cut me to the core. It's like he's making fun of me for taking this seriously.

"Well, I don't want to go, okay?" I snap. I sit down on my bed and pull my legs up tight against my chest. "I really should head home. I have a lot of studying to do tonight. My first final is coming up in a few days, and I'm not ready for it."

"Bailey," he says. "Let's talk about this."

"I have to go."

I hang up, tears welling up in my eyes for the first time all week. I have no idea why I just snapped at him like that, but now he probably thinks I'm a jerk. Or a total mental case.

I jump when the phone rings again. It's Judd calling back, but I don't think I can face him right now. I'm embarrassed and upset and scared. I send the call to voicemail and silence the ringer. Just to be extra safe, I stuff the phone under my pillow and disappear into the bathroom, letting the tears fall until I calm myself down enough to head back into the living room to face Monica. It's the first time I've cried all week.

"What happened?" she asks, a huge smile on her face. Then she sees my red eyes and frowns. "Whoa, seriously, what happened?"

I shrug. "I don't even know," I say, half-laughing. "He asked me to go hang out tonight with his friends, and I completely freaked out for no reason."

She bites her lip. "You don't want to meet his friends?"

"I don't want to be judged by his friends," I say. "It's been so nice being able to just be myself around him, you know? There are no games between us. No crazy drama or lies or pretension. Well, except when I cause the drama. When we're together, we can be honest and silly and fun. I don't even know what kind of friends he has. I wouldn't know how to act."

Monica sits up straighter in her chair. "Well, doesn't it make sense that if you can be yourself around Judd that you could probably just be yourself around his friends? I mean, he likes you for who you are. You don't have to impress his friends to get him to approve of you, if that's what you're worried about."

The tears begin to fall again, and I swipe at them, then

grab my plate and take it into the kitchen. I throw half of my sandwich into the trash, my appetite completely gone.

Monica follows close behind me. "Bailey, you don't have to explain yourself to me," she says. She throws her arms around me and I hug her back, not even sure why I'm crying. "If you aren't ready to meet his friends, you just aren't."

"Thanks," I say, but deep down, I know I'm being stupid and irrational.

I think about my phone in the other room and wonder if Judd has tried to call again. I wonder what I'd say to him even if he is still willing to talk to me.

I pull away from my friend and snag a clean napkin from the counter. I wipe my eyes and blow my nose.

"Better?" she asks.

I nod and am about to suggest we head out to the library to study when someone knocks on the door.

Monica eyes me, one eyebrow raised. "Are you expecting someone?" she asks.

I shake my head, my hands trembling slightly. "You don't think he'd come all the way over here, do you?"

She lifts her palms. "I have no clue. You're the one who knows the guy. Would he?"

"Maybe," I say. My heart is racing. "You answer it."

I'm such a coward.

I hide in the kitchen while Monica walks to the door. I lean my head against the cool wallpaper and wait, unsure if I want it to be him or not.

Then I hear his voice and I know. I wanted it to be him all along.

CHAPTER 19

"**I**s Bailey here?"

I can't tell if he sounds angry or just anxious.

I look at the clock. It can't have been more than fifteen minutes since he called. Did he seriously just get in his car and come over here because I wouldn't answer the phone?

"Ummm..." Monica stalls like a good friend, probably waiting to see if I want him to know I'm here or not.

Nervous, I step around the corner. "I'm here," I say softly.

His eyes seek mine. It's possible he's a little bit angry. His face is tense and he definitely does not look happy.

I feel like a child who has suddenly been caught doing something bad.

"Can I talk to you for a second?" he asks.

Monica turns around and squeezes my hand as she walks past me and back toward her bedroom. God bless that girl. She's a true friend.

"Do you want to come in?" I ask.

Judd walks in and shuts the door behind him. He pulls his coat off and lays it on the back of the couch. He runs a hand through his wavy hair.

"What the fuck was that about?" he asks. He isn't yelling at me, but from his tight jaw, he seems to be struggling to hold it together.

I may have been feeling embarrassed and ashamed before he walked through the door, but the anger in his tone sets me on the defensive.

"I told you it seemed like a big step and you..." I can't finish my explanation. When I say it out loud, it sounds completely stupid.

"I what? Told you it wasn't a big deal? Okay, so let's talk about that," he says. "It's just my friends. These are the people I hang out with when I have free time and I've been dying for them to meet you. What's the problem there?"

I cross my arms in front of my chest and back toward the wall. I'm not used to being spoken to so directly. I don't know what to say to him.

"Bailey, you need to talk to me," he says. "I'm trying really hard to understand why, after an entire week of spending as much time together as possible, you would get upset, hang up and then refuse to answer your phone."

My mouth drops open, but I still don't have a response. I turn my face away from him, feeling childish and awful.

He paces the space behind the couch. "Is there something else wrong?" he asks. "Because I hate playing games, Bailey. I despise it. I don't like to be manipulated or lied to, so if practically hanging up on me is your version of trying to get me to do something you want, you need to tell me to my face what it is. I don't want to have to start trying to read between the lines with you."

I do everything I can to hold back my tears, but it's no use. I don't really know how to react to this. I'm not used to just saying what I mean or what I'm feeling. "I wasn't trying to manipulate you," I say, the tears obvious in my voice. "I was trying to tell you that to me, meeting your friends is a really big step."

"Okay," he says, leaning against the back of the couch. "Explain that to me."

I shrug. "I have no idea who they are," I say. "I don't know what kind of people they are or what they expect from me."

He narrows his eyes at me, his lips parting slightly. "I don't understand what you mean," he says. "They don't expect anything from you."

My face tenses and my head pounds. "I don't know how to explain it without sounding stupid," I say, wiping the tears from my eyes. "I'm scared that your friends won't like me, okay? What if I wear the wrong clothes or I don't fit in? What if they don't think I'm right for you? Then what?"

He shakes his head and walks toward me. "Is that seriously what you're worried about? That my friends won't approve of you?"

I nod and sniff, turning away so he won't see me crying.

But he takes my shoulders in his strong hands and gently turns me back to face him. "Bailey, you don't have to worry about that for one second," he says. "I like you. That's all that matters to them. Trust me. They'll love you."

For some reason, that only makes me cry harder. "You don't know that," I say.

"Yes I do," he says softly. He pushes my hair back from my face and cups my cheek. "And even if they don't, it's not going to make any difference to me. I already care about you too much to worry about what they think."

I sniff again and look up to meet his gaze. "You do?"

He nods and smiles, then kisses my forehead. "Yes," he says. "I thought you already knew that."

I shake my head and turn toward his hand, kissing his palm. "I'm sorry," I whisper. "I kind of freaked out."

"I could tell," he says with a laugh. "But next time you freak out can you just talk to me about it instead of hanging up and refusing to answer my calls?"

I nod. "I still can't believe you came all the way over here."

I'm so used to playing games with Preston. Hanging up to try to get him to understand that he's made me angry. Or to get him to agree to something I want. Waiting to see how long it will take him to show up at my doorstep with roses.

Judd's right, in a way, I was trying to manipulate him.

I never expected him to drive straight here and call me on it.

"Communication is the one thing that matters most to me," he says. "No games or secrets, okay? I know it's only been a week, but I really like you, Bailey. I really think there could be something special between us if we give it a chance."

"I like you, too," I say. "I'm sorry I didn't answer the phone."

He leans down and kisses both my cheeks, then plants a soft kiss on my lips. "You can always just be honest with me," he says. "I hope you know that."

"I do," I say.

"Besides, if I hadn't come over here, I might have missed seeing the Christmas spectacle that is this apartment."

I look around and giggle. Compared to his sad little tree, our apartment is like a winter wonderland. There are Christmas decorations covering nearly ever surface in the room. "What can I say? We like Christmas. Don't you?"

"It's quickly becoming my favorite time of year," he whispers, drawing me in to another kiss.

CHAPTER 20

No matter how many times Judd tries to convince me that it doesn't matter what I wear tonight, I still end up spending an hour and a half stressing over my closet.

When I was hanging out with my friends from high school, I always had to think about what I was wearing. Penny was always super sweet, but Krystal and Summer would give me shit if I was wearing something that wasn't in season or "nice" enough for the occasion. Keeping up with their wardrobes was exhausting. I don't even know if they realized how much their snide little comments about my outfits really got to me sometimes.

My family isn't poor by any means, but we also aren't anywhere near the level of families like Preston and Penny's.

Buying a new pair of two hundred dollar jeans was nothing for someone like Summer, but for me it was more than a full week's worth of shifts at The Cup. None of them ever had to work, so they never seemed to understand what it was like for me.

I have no idea what to expect when it comes to Judd's friends. Are they rich like Summer and the others? Are they super down-to-earth like Judd?

My mother always says that first impressions are the most important, and even though Judd says he'll still like me no matter what, I want to make a good impression with his friends.

Monica helps me some before she has to head out to work for the evening, and we finally settle on a black skirt with a red long-sleeve button-up shirt that accentuates my boobs. My black boots. Simple jewelry.

When Judd knocks on the door promptly at six, I grab my leather jacket and head out the door.

"Whoa," he says, taking my appearance in from head-to-toe. "Maybe we should just stay in tonight."

My heart sinks and I look down at my choice of outfit. Did I do something wrong? "What? Should I change?"

He shakes his head and pulls me into his arms. "No. It's just that you look so good, I don't know how I'm going to be able to keep my hands off you," he says.

I smile and lift up, pressing my lips against his. They're warm despite the cold evening air.

"Come to think of it, maybe staying in isn't such a bad idea," I say, kissing him again.

"Oh no," he says, taking my hand and leading me toward the stairs. "You're not getting out of this that easy."

I groan and follow him to his car.

"You have nothing to worry about. Trust me," he says. "And if you're not having a good time, we can leave."

Judd holds my hand all the way to his friend's house, and by the time we pull up to the small brick house, my heart has somewhat settled into a normal rhythm.

Of course, the second I get out of the car, it's racing again and I feel like I can barely swallow.

There are at least eight cars parked in front of the small house and when Judd opens the front door, Christmas music and laughter spills out into the night air.

He squeezes my hand and we walk inside, following the sounds toward the kitchen.

There's a crowd of people standing around the island and lounging against the countertops, their hands filled with food and red Solo cups. When they see us, a collective shout goes up and several people come over to give him a hug or to shake his hand in that half-slap, half-grasp kind of way guy friends do.

"Judd, welcome my friend," a tall guy with bright red hair says, slapping him on the back. "Who is this goddess you have here?"

I almost look around like an idiot. Is he talking about me?

"This is the girl I was telling you about," he says. "Bailey, this is my friend Brian. He's a first-year law student."

Brian takes my hand and gives it a little kiss. I can't help but giggle.

"Hi Bailey, I'm Tess, Brian's fiance." A short girl with a dark pixie cut steps forward to shake my hand. "We're glad you could make it. Judd's told us a lot about you."

She raises an eyebrow at Judd like they share some special secret, and I wonder what in the world that's about. Besides, how much could he really have told them? We've only been going out for a week.

"Thanks," I say. "Thanks for having me."

Judd takes me around the room, introducing me to his friends. I already know I won't remember everyone's names, but so far they're all super nice.

I feel a little awkward at first. These people all seem to know each other so well. I stick close to Judd's side as we stand in the kitchen snacking on the food that's spread out across the counters. Fruit. Veggies. Meatballs. Lots of finger foods.

Tess brings me a glass of her famous homemade eggnog, and after we've been here about half an hour, I start to relax.

I'm actually a little bit overdressed, but no one seems to care or even notice. I get the distinct feeling they would treat me the same way whether I was wearing this or my sweats.

It's a foreign concept to me for a party, but I relax into it, glad to not feel like I'm under scrutiny or being judged.

After a while, the group migrates toward the living room and someone jokes about Judd's dancing skills.

I cut my eyes toward him and I swear he actually blushes.

"Let's not subject Bailey to that just yet," he says. "She doesn't need to know every embarrassing thing about me."

"Wait," I say. "I have to know what you guys are talking about. He's actually blushing. This has to be good."

Brian laughs, clutching his stomach. "Oh, it is," he says. "It's epic."

I smile, dying to know what they're talking about. Judd and I danced together that first night at the bar, but I don't think that's quite what they're talking about here.

"Guys, let's just let it go," Judd says, but he's laughing just as hard as Brian is.

One of the other guys, Axel, puts his hand on my shoulder. "Bailey, my dear, by the end of this evening, you'll either be completely in love with this guy or running the other way," he says.

"Running," another guy tosses out.

"I have to know what this is all about," I say to Judd.

"One," he says, holding up a single finger and shrugging out of his jacket. "I'll do one. Then it's someone else's turn. I refuse to be the subject of everyone's jokes again tonight."

I'm so thoroughly confused until someone brings out an Xbox controller and turns on the television.

Tess grabs my hand and pulls me out of the center of the room. We find a spot on the couch, which I notice now has been pulled to the side to leave the floor clear.

When the TV comes on, the logo for a game called Just Dance comes across the screen, and I bring my hand to my mouth to hide my smile. Judd is going to dance to this game? Oh, this is going to be good.

"Girlfriend's choice," Brian says.

I suddenly realize he's looking at me and I swallow. Girlfriend?

I must look like a deer caught in headlights, because Judd clears his throat and smacks Brian across the chest.

"Oh, um, Bailey, pick a song. Any song."

I try not to act rattled and turn my attention to the choices on the screen. It's not that I'm totally against the idea of becoming Judd's girlfriend, but we haven't even talked about that yet. Can you become someone's girlfriend after just a week of dating? I honestly don't even know what's normal or expected.

Brian is scrolling through the choices when I point to the screen. "Wait, back up," I say. "Justin Bieber. For sure."

Judd groans.

"Hey, my choice," I say, teasing.

His eyes meet mine and he smiles. My stomach flips and butterflies dance around deep inside. God, I love that smile.

The music begins and Judd shifts his eyes toward the screen.

I watch him in awe. I can't believe how free he is. He completely misses most of the moves, but he doesn't even seem to care that he looks like a fool. Whenever he does happen to get a perfect move, the whole room erupts in loud cheers and Judd throws his fist in the air, which then always makes him miss the next few moves.

By the time the song is over, I'm laughing so hard, I might pee my pants. I completely forget the fact that I'm supposed to be nervous around his friends.

When the song is over, Judd's score comes up. Two stars. He turns around and cheers. "Two stars," he shouts, pumping his fist. "YES."

I stand and clap and he comes over and lifts me up into his arms, twirling me around. He plants a deep kiss on my lips.

I pull away in surprise. Preston never kissed me in front of his friends. He said he wasn't into PDA. It was always one of the things I hated most about our relationship. In private, he was all mine. But in public, he was never comfortable showing any kind of affection.

Judd stares into my eyes, still holding my feet off the

ground and not seeming to care that all his friends are watching us.

"Your turn," he says.

I realize he's talking about the game and for a moment, I think I might die. But then I think, what the hell, right?

My heart races. "Only if you do it with me," I say.

He nods and the people around us cheer and laugh. I sit down on the couch and unzip my boots, then toss them to the side of the room.

I smile and laugh and let go, feeling the walls around my heart bend and break and open.

CHAPTER 21

I t's almost midnight by the time Judd and I say goodbye to his friends. My cheeks hurt from smiling and laughing so much and I've had just enough eggnog throughout the evening to keep a very light buzz going.

When Judd takes my hand and pulls me in for a kiss just outside the door, an entirely different kind of buzz begins.

Our make-out sessions have been increasingly passionate as the week has gone on, and I honestly don't know how much longer I can resist the temptation to rip his clothes off.

"I told you you'd love my friends," he says as he leads me to his car.

"I really did have a great time," I say. "I had no idea your friends would be so cool."

He smiles and my heart races. His eyes dip to my lips and desire flashes across his features. He stops beside the passenger door to his car and turns me around so that my back is pressed against the cold frame.

He doesn't say a word. He just places his warm hands on

either side of my face and draws me toward him, our breath mingling as our lips meet, our mouths opening and closing in hurried need. I want him in a way I never expected. There are no walls between us right now. He's seen more of me in the past week than I've ever let any guy see my whole life.

The fact that I don't have to put on pretenses around him or play games to try to get him to notice me is one of the sexiest things about him.

He likes me for me.

And, oh God, I like everything about him, too.

I slide my hands beneath his jacket, drawing his shirt into my fists, pulling him closer.

He moans and buries his hands deep in my hair. Our lips separate and I kiss a pattern along his jaw and down his neck, wishing we weren't standing on a public street where anyone could see.

"Please tell me you don't have to work tomorrow," he says.

My body reacts to the implication with a warm sensation deep down.

"Not until noon," I say.

He moans again and draws my mouth back to his. He grinds his hips against me and I can feel him growing hard. I press into him, grabbing at his belt loops.

"I'm really trying to be a gentleman, here," he says, breathless between kisses. "But I'm not sure how much longer I can keep it up."

I smile and kiss the hard line of his jaw. "Then don't," I whisper.

He shivers and looks down, his hazel eyes lit with desire.

"I don't want to rush you," he says. "I know it's only been a week, but—"

"If you're not ready—"

"I didn't say that." A corner of his mouth lifts in a sly smile. He still has his hands firmly cradling my neck and face. "I just want to make sure it's what you want. I don't want anything to mess this up, Bailey."

I breathe in, my heart racing. I want him so badly, but I'm also scared. If I'm already liking him this much, what is sleeping with him going to do? If he breaks my heart now, I don't know if I'll recover. One heartbreak is bad enough. Two in short succession would kill me.

And I'm honestly not sure I'm really over the first one yet.

Which complicates things.

"I'll take you home," he says, his voice catching on the words. He lowers his hand to mine and squeezes once, then moves to open my door for me.

I push the door closed and grab his jacket with both hands, pulling him toward me. "I don't want to go home."

He swallows. His eyes explore my face. "Are you sure?"

"I'm sure," I say. My knees grow weak and my adrenaline is pumping. I don't know if I'm doing the right thing by trusting him with my heart, but I'm tired of always being careful and plotting these things out. I thought I had the rest of my life planned out with Preston and look where that got me.

This time, I'm not going to follow some master plan, figuring out each step before I've even given a single thought to what I really want.

This time, I'm going to follow my heart.

CHAPTER 22

I can't keep my hands off of him as he throws open the door to his apartment and ushers me inside.

My arms go up and around his neck and he pulls his jacket off and tosses it to the floor. He reaches both hands up to cup my cheeks, his lips exploring mine in a torrid rush of heat.

He pushes my back against the wall of the front hallway, then moves his hand down to help me out of my coat. His fingertips explore the soft curves of my sweater, caressing me and touching me in a way that builds a swelling need between my thighs.

There's entirely too much fabric between us still, and I want it off so I can touch his hard body and his warm skin. In all our making out so far, we've stayed completely above clothes and mainly just spent hours kissing.

But I want so much more tonight.

All I can think about is exploring him, tasting him, feeling his hands all over me.

I grab his shirt into my fist and kneed his back, pulling him closer. I pull the shirt up and slide my other hand under, moaning at the warmth of his skin on my palm. He mirrors my movements, slipping his hand beneath the edge of my sweater and running his hands up and down across my back.

It's nowhere near enough.

I push him away and cross my arms over my body, reaching for the bottom of my sweater. In one swift motion, I pull the sweater over my head, our eyes locked the entire time. Slowly, hungrily, he lets his eyes travel downward. His breath is fast and shallow as he takes in my barely-covered breasts.

I step forward and tug at the edge of his shirt, pulling it upward. He finishes the task, in a crossing and uncrossing of his arms, his face disappearing only for a brief moment as his shirt disappears, revealing the rock solid cut of muscles underneath.

His stomach and chest move with the force of his breath and when I reach out to run my finger along the trail of fine blond hair leading downward, his breath hitches and his stomach trembles.

He grips my hand tightly and pulls me toward the bedroom. We leave a trail of clothing as we kiss our way down the hall. My skirt. His jeans. Boots. Shoes. Socks.

By the time we are standing beside the bed, we're down to nothing more than underwear.

I reach for the light switch, but he shakes his head.

"I want to see you," he says.

I bite my lower lip. I definitely want to see him, too, but I'm nervous about feeling so vulnerable in front of him. Now that we've reached the point where the more intimate touching naturally begins, I'm drawing back, scared of these feelings swelling within me.

My legs tremble and no matter how hard I try, I can't seem to draw in a complete breath.

He approaches me slowly, tenderly. He pushes my hair back from my face and with a touch as soft as a whisper, he runs his fingertips down my cheeks, my neck, and over the swell of my breasts. He navigates to my back and unhooks my bra, then brings his hands to my shoulders, slowly pushing the straps down and off until my chest is bare.

My nipples harden as his eyes flash with desire.

He continues his soft exploration, moving his hands up and around my breasts, then over the top of my nipples. I moan and let my lips fall apart. My chest thumps with every beat of my pounding heart.

I stand there, still on the outside but pulsing with need on the inside, as he moves his hands lower. My head falls back as he drags his fingers across my hips and down my thighs.

He steps closer and the warmth of his body radiates toward me. Parts of him touch me, but he doesn't press. He leaves enough space for his hands to continue caressing me.

I can't keep mine still any longer, so I lift them up to his body, touching him with the same tenderness he's shown me.

Desire grows between us, swelling like a giant wave headed toward the shore.

And when his fingers finally, mercifully, slide between my thighs and slip into the wetness there, the wave breaks over us and we are lost to it.

His mouth finds mine and as he presses his body against me, I'm overwhelmed with a thousand beautiful sensations.

His hands rubbing me. My breasts pressing against his chest. Our lips tasting each other. The length of him expanding against me, growing harder with every touch.

I bring my trembling hand up to stroke him and he breaths in, his body tensing. A low sound forms deep in his chest and he drives his fingers inside of me.

I have lost control and inhibition. I am reduced to want and need and the beautiful ache between my legs.

When he lays me down across the bed, I swallow hard, my eyes drinking in the sight of his body as he stands there naked in front of me.

He reaches into the top drawer of the nightstand beside the bed and pulls out a condom. My breath is heavy and my legs writhe against the sheets as I watch him stretch it over the length of him. He looks up and our eyes meet. There's a thrilling charge in the air between us. A magnetic pull that draws us together.

He moves onto the bed, his hands resting on my knees, then slowly spreading my thighs to give him access. His eyes devour me and I lift my hand to my face, embarrassed and aroused at the same time.

He opens me wider, then positions himself above me. He takes my hand in his and moves it away from my face. Up and over my head.

"You are the most beautiful woman I've ever seen," he says. His voice is gruff and I realize this is the first we've talked since we walked in the door of his apartment.

He takes my mouth with his, passion surging with each new kiss.

I hook my legs around his hips and lift up toward him, wanting him more than I ever knew was possible.

I feel the tip of him at the edge of my wetness and I moan. I bury my hands in his hair and pull him closer, filled with something beyond need. Something more. As if my survival depended on it.

When he enters me, he moves slowly. I open my mouth against his, inhaling as my body stretches to accommodate him. He teases me, moving in and out at the edge of my sex, never quite giving me his entire length until I cry out and bite his shoulder, my mind spinning.

Finally, he reaches the end of his restraint and thrusts deeper, our bodies becoming one. We move in unison, finding a rhythm that quickens and becomes more desperate with each push.

Pleasure builds within me as he enters me and I dig my fingers into his back. I feel him tense and together, we tumble over the edge in a moment of complete surrender and release.

We hold each other long after we've climaxed, letting our breathing slow and our heartbeats pulse against each other's skin. He showers me with soft kisses and I trace lazy circles on his glistening skin.

We fall asleep in each other's arms, our bodies spent and trembling.

CHAPTER 23

I wake and stretch, elongating my body until the tips of my toes curl and a yawn begins. Then I open my eyes and remember where I am.

My body tingles as I remember last night's love making. I've never had sex like that before. It was so beautiful. A true give and take. I wasn't worried about whether I would please him or if he wanted me. I knew it without him having to say a word.

I pull the covers close against my body and study the empty spot beside me in the bed. I sit up and listen. I smell coffee brewing and in the kitchen, I can hear Judd stirring things and...humming?

I smile and search the floor for my clothes. I wish I'd anticipated spending the night with him. I would have at least thrown a change of clothes and some basic makeup into my bag. My purse must be somewhere in the living room, but I think the only thing I have in there is lipgloss anyway.

I breathe into my hand and sniff. Ugh. Morning breath. And my hair is probably atrocious. I can't let him see me like this.

I briefly consider trying to sneak out the front door, but I know that's ridiculous. I close my eyes and collapse back into the pillows.

God, I had such an amazing time last night. It almost doesn't seem real. I keep waiting for the bad news. No one's this perfect.

I snuggle into the covers and catch a whiff of his cologne. I bring his pillow to my face and bury my head in it, my legs shaking at the familiar scent that is now closely tied to the memory of an earth-shattering orgasm.

Judd's laughter carries across the room and I practically throw his pillow.

"Were you just smelling my pillow?" he asks.

I cut my eyes over to him and nearly have the breath knocked out of me. He's wearing nothing but a pair of pj bottoms that hang low on his waist. A trail of blond hair runs down his chest and I follow it down to his waistband, my mouth going dry at the sight of his perfect, hard body in the light of day.

He pushes his hair back behind his ear on one side and smiles. "Totally busted," he says. He walks to the end of the bed and climbs up toward me.

I giggle and hide myself inside the covers.

He yanks them from me and lays down on top of me. I'm completely naked except for my panties. I have almost zero makeup on and my long hair is knotted to hell.

But the way he looks at me takes my breath away.

There is no judgment in his eyes. No criticism. Only adoration.

"How is it possible you look even more beautiful this morning than ever?" he says, running his finger along my jawline.

I turn my head, wanting to hide under something. But there's nowhere to hide. I'm completely exposed. "I look gross and my breath stinks," I say.

He shakes his head. "You're stunning."

I swallow hard, my heart pounding against his arm draped across my chest.

He lowers his lips to mine. I pull away, suddenly feeling more vulnerable than ever. There's something stirring between us that's deeper than just a fling or a casual relationship. This is way more. My stomach twists, and I'm not sure I'm ready for this.

I try to climb off the bed, but he doesn't let me run away. "Hey," he says. "What's wrong?"

I shrug and push him off so I can sit up. My throat feels like it's closing up all of a sudden. I feel claustrophobic and enclosed in this room.

"I should probably get dressed and head home so I can shower and get ready for work."

He sits up and watches me as I scramble to pick up my scattered clothing. "It's only eight in the morning," he says. "You've got hours before you have to be at work."

I shake my head so my hair will drape over my face. I feel like I can't breathe.

"I know, but I have to shower and I really should try to get some studying in before."

He doesn't say anything, but I feel the atmosphere in the

room shift. I look up and see nothing but pure disappointment in his expression. Maybe the small hint of fear.

He moves to the edge of the bed and stands up. He takes my hand. "Did I do something wrong?"

"No," I say, meeting his eyes so he'll know I mean it. "Last night was amazing. I'm just..."

I don't finish that thought. I can't explain how I'm feeling. It's uncomfortable. Uncertain.

Fucking terrified.

"So stay," he says. "I'm making breakfast. I thought we could hang out for a while this morning, then tonight I could come by The Cup when you get off work."

I step away, not even sure why I'm doing it. But suddenly I'm scared. I'm a cornered rabbit and I just need to run. This room feels very small and hot and I can't breathe.

"I'm sorry," I say, backing toward the bathroom.

I dress as fast as I can, my heart going back and forth between the bravery I felt last night and the fear I've lived with the other 21 years of my life.

I know I'm stupid for not melting into his kisses this morning, but something about the way he told me I was beautiful scared the shit out of me. The way he looked at me. The way he touched me. Like he could see the deepest parts of me.

Like he loved me.

I'm used to having a safe buffer between me and my emotions. I'm used to being able to sit back and think about how I want things to go. With Judd, it's all instinct and in the moment. It's raw. And it's real. There's no time to think and I'm not sure I can do this. It feels dangerous.

I brush my hair with his brush, throw my clothes on, and

head back out. He's in the kitchen leaning against the counter with a cup of coffee in his hand. He put on a t-shirt and it feels like just another layer between us. My heart aches for the freedom I felt last night. I wish I could be that person for him now.

"I can't even talk you into a cup of coffee?" he asks.

I frown and shake my head. "No thanks," I say. "I had a really great time last night, though."

"Did you?" he asks.

My head snaps up. Oh God, he's going to do that honesty thing again. I glance toward the door, wondering how fast I could get there from here. I need time to think through what I'm feeling before I can talk about it.

"Yes," I say, brightening my tone, trying to fake him out. "Of course I did."

He narrows his eyes. "Because last night didn't feel like this," he says. "Last night was...really you and really me, you know? Then all of a sudden, there's this wall here between us. What happened?"

I swallow. "I'm sorry. I'm used to a relationship with walls," I say. "This is new for me and I need for you to give me some time."

"Okay," he says.

Tears spring to my eyes. "I'm sorry," I say. There's so much more in my heart that I want to tell him, but I'm scared he'll think I'm crazy. I'm scared it won't make any different and will just open myself up to more pain. "I'll talk to you later."

I walk over and lift up on my toes to give him a soft kiss on the cheek.

He's tense and doesn't smile or move to kiss me back.

I turn, a familiar heaviness in the pit of my stomach as I walk through the front door, putting yet another wall between us. It doesn't hit me until I'm pulling into the parking lot at my apartment that somewhere along the way last night, I stopped comparing him to Preston.

CHAPTER 24

All day I watch the door, waiting to see Judd walk in with that smile on his face. Wanting him to appear as if I hadn't acted like a complete and total bitch to him this morning.

But as the hours stretch on, I start to lose hope. On a break, I check my phone. No messages or texts.

I want to punch myself in the face. What the hell did I do?

I freaked out, that's what.

I knew I'd made a huge mistake by the time I got to my apartment this morning, but I couldn't work up the nerve to turn back and knock on his door to apologize. He was nothing but amazing last night and this morning, and I treated him like crap.

I wouldn't be surprised if he never wants to talk to me again.

I bite my lip and start a text to him.

I'm sorry about this morning. Are you still coming by

The Cup?

I stare at it for a full minute before I send it. My hands are trembling. What if he says no? Or is distant from now on? What if I've ruined everything and have to spend the rest of my life haunted by how perfect last night was for us?

I knew I shouldn't have slept with him. It was just too soon for me. I wasn't expecting it to mean so much. I thought I was more closed off. More protected.

But Judd has brought down more of my barriers than I thought.

In the dark of night, it felt great. But in the light of day, I just felt exposed and vulnerable.

Please don't let it be too late to fix it.

It's close to the end of my shift and I've pretty much given up on Judd showing up to hang out when the bell over the door sounds. I breathe in, my heart racing as I turn.

My mouth falls open and my breath catches in my throat.

Preston's eyes meet mine across the small cafe. Seeing him right now is like a punch to my gut. What is he doing here? From the way he's looking at me, I know he's here to see me, but why? It's like guys have this sixth sense about things like this. It's like they know the moment you've started to move on so they swoop in and surprise you, hoping to sweep your feet out from under you. Ex-boyfriends seem to know just how to hit you when you're down.

I wipe my sweaty hands on my apron and force a smile as he walks over.

He kisses my cheek. "Hey," he says. "It's been a while."

I nod and smile, holding it together by a thread. "Yeah," I say. "What brings you in here?"

"Oh," he says, pulling his hands from his pockets. "The

Christmas Memories Ball next weekend. You didn't forget, did you? I kept meaning to call, but things have been crazy busy."

My heart stops and dizziness washes over me. What is he saying?

"I just stopped by to give you the details on the plan," he says, as if it's just completely normal that he's talking to me about this for the first time in weeks.

"O-of course," I stutter, completely caught off guard. I grab the side of the table to steady myself. My ears are ringing and huge warning sirens are going off in my brain.

"There will be six of us in the limo," he says. "Penny and Mason were going to join us, but she wants to get there ahead of time, so it'll just be us, Summer and Ben, and Krystal and Park."

I'm in shock. I can't speak, so he just keeps rattling off details like it's no big deal.

"Would you rather come by my place before or should I have the limo swing by your place to pick you up? Or did you have plans to meet up with Summer and Krystal first?"

My mouth is just hanging open. I have no words.

"Is everything okay?" he asks. His face goes white and his eyes widen. "You were still planning to go, right? We made these plans ages ago."

I shake my head, finally finding my voice. "Preston, I don't know what to say." My heart is urging me to tell him I can't go, that I've met someone else, but I can't seem to form the words in my mouth. I'm trapped. "I didn't realize you were still planning on taking me. I figured—"

"Shit," he says, running a hand through his dark brown hair, which is a little longer on top than normal. It looks really good on him, and I hate myself for even thinking it. "I'm sorry Bailey, I should have called or something, but I just assumed we were still on for this. I'm really counting on you coming with me."

I breathe in and out through my nose, unable to think clearly.

"Sure," I say. "Of course I'm still going. What time again?"

He smiles, but I want to cry. I never could say no to anything he asked of me. It's a sickness, really. I have no idea how I'm going to tell Judd. Maybe things are over between Judd and I anyway.

"Everyone's coming to my place around five," he says. "Then the limo is supposed to be there around five-thirty to take us to dinner at Ray's. The dance starts at seven."

I nod and press my lips together.

"So you'll come by my place?"

"Whatever works best for you," I say, smiling. I think of how Judd's apartment looks out over the parking lot. How am I going to explain this to him? This is turning into a huge mess, but I can't bring myself to say no to Preston. It's a long-learned habit, impossible to break no matter how much he hurt me.

"Okay, then, I'll see you around five at my apartment," he says. He takes my hand in his and his thumb caresses mine. "I'm looking forward to spending some time with you."

I stand there staring after him for several minutes before I finally pull myself together enough to clean the rest of the tables and close out my shift. I don't even know what to make of that. Is he really looking forward to spending time with me? Or is that just something you say to your ex-girlfriend when you need her to do something for you?

And how am I going to break this to Judd? Will he care? Or is he mad at me already?

I glance at the clock and realize my shift should have ended fifteen minutes ago. He never came in like he said he would, anyway. There are no messages on my phone, either.

I clock out and pull my coat tight against my body. I walk the whole way home in the cold evening air, unsure of what I want anymore.

CHAPTER 25

I try Judd's cell phone a few more times, but he never picks up and he never calls back.

Maybe it's for the best. We had one amazing week together. One unbelievable night together. And now it's over. He gave me just enough to make me realize there's hope for my future, but we don't have to go through the painful parts of a relationship that come later.

But even as I'm saying this to myself, I know it's complete bullshit.

If I can never be with him again, it's going to hurt.

Bad.

I'm falling for him. Yes, I got scared this morning, but isn't he the one who said we should talk through these kinds of things? Well, if he wants to talk, he'll call.

And if not, then I'll move on. I'll find a way to get up every day and keep breathing.

Over the next few days, I have to give myself constant pep talks to keep from completely falling apart. I stopped calling and texting him, sick of feeling desperate. The whole thing reminds me of how things went with Preston after the summer. It was always me chasing and him running away.

I can't go through that again.

I throw myself into my studies, head to my final classes and do the best I can on the exams. My statistics test was the worst, and it'll be a miracle if I passed, but everything else seemed to go alright.

In order to keep myself from falling back into my old pattern of sleeping all day and crying every waking moment, I spend a lot of time in the art studio, working on a new painting.

I'm scrubbing red paint off my fingers with scalding hot water when Monica pokes her head into my bathroom doorway on Wednesday afternoon.

"Heya," she says. "Any news?"

I shake my head. "Nothing," I say.

She frowns. "I really thought this guy was different," she says. "I don't get it."

"You and me both," I say, holding back tears. "I guess I freaked him out by the way I acted the other morning and he just doesn't want to see me again."

She grips the edge of the doorframe. "I don't know. I still think it's weird," she says. "Especially after he rushed right over here the second you didn't answer your phone that one day. Hey, maybe he's just waiting for you to come by his place?"

I lift my head, wondering if that's what I should do. Should I fight for this? Should I make him listen to my apology and see what he has to say for himself?

My stomach feels sick just thinking about it. "I've got to

go to work for a few hours this afternoon," I say. "Maybe I'll try stopping by his apartment after that. If he doesn't talk to me, then at least I'll know it's over for good."

Monica sighs. "I really thought he was special."

"Me too," I say again. I wipe my clean hands on a towel, then get dressed for work and head out into the cold afternoon.

CHAPTER 26

My shift is only a couple of hours long, so it goes by quickly.

I still have this brief moment of hope every time the bell jingles over the door, but it's always followed by a sinking disappointment when it's not Judd.

When I head out, I hear my name on the wind and turn to see Preston walking toward me across the grass.

I stop and wait for him to catch up to me.

"Hi," I say. "How are finals going?"

He shrugs and sticks his hands into the pockets of his expensive leather jacket. "Courses have been pretty easy this year," he says. "It's next semester I'm worried about. Trying to juggle the internship with a full course load is going to be tough."

"I'm sure," I say. Silence falls between us and it strikes me how much we've changed in the past month. How much I've changed.

We stand together a few more minutes making meaningless small talk and then he reaches for my hand.

"I'm really glad you're still going to the dance on Saturday," he says.

I wonder briefly about the blond pony-tail girl I saw him talking to that day last week. I wonder why he isn't taking her instead. But it's none of my business, and in some ways, I'm really glad to at least be able to wear the dress I sacrificed so much to pay for.

Preston leans forward and plants a soft kiss on my forehead. I close my eyes, breathing in his familiar scent. I used to love that scent, but now there's a different one that trumps this.

A tear falls down my cheek and I pull away, swiping at it.

"Bailey—" he starts.

I press my hand against his chest, stopping him. "Don't," I say. "Just let it go."

I don't tell him this tear isn't for him. I'm crying for someone else. For what might have been if I hadn't screwed it up.

And when I look away, I think I've imagined him into existence. Judd is standing less than fifty feet away, staring straight at us.

I almost don't believe he's real, but the anger and sorrow on his face is definitely real.

He turns abruptly and heads toward the science building.

"I'm sorry," I tell Preston. "I have to go."

"I'll see you Saturday then," he says.

I nod and wave, but take off in a run toward Judd. I catch him just before he hits the steps heading up to the entrance.

I have to call his name twice before he finally turns around, and when he does, I'm not quite sure what to say.

We stand there, just staring at each other for a moment until I find my words.

"I've been calling you," I say.

"I know," he says, swallowing. His eyes dart toward where Preston and I were standing.

I take a deep breath, wanting so badly to be good at just being honest about how I feel. "Listen, I know I really screwed up the other morning, but you have to understand that I'm still really fresh off a breakup with a guy that I dated for years," I say.

This is hard for me. Being direct and honest even when I know some of the things I might say can be hurtful or embarrassing. But I want to try. For him.

"That night, it was amazing." I step toward him, but he backs away as if I'm a poisonous snake. The motion rocks me. Disrupts my thoughts. I clear my throat. "I—"

"I can't do this," he says.

My eyebrows come together in a frown. "Can't do what?"

"I can't go through this again," he says. He looks toward where Preston is still standing, talking to a friend. "I overheard someone saying the two of you are going to a party together on Saturday."

I breathe in. "Yes," I say. "There's this charity ball the Wrights throw every year."

"And you're going with him? As his date? When were you going to tell me about it?" he asks. He pushes the sleeves of his coat up and shifts his weight.

"I didn't think—"

He holds his hand up and turns his head to the side. "You

know what, I don't want to hear it," he says. He glances at his watch, his teeth clenched. "I have to go. I'm sorry."

"Wait," I say, chasing after him. "Let's talk about this."

He shakes his head, walking backward toward the door of the building. "I don't think I have anything left to say to you."

His words nail my feet to the concrete steps.

I can't move. I can only stare blankly forward as he disappears into the science building, tears streaming down my face.

I don't even understand what just happened between us, but it's obvious he wants nothing more to do with me. My heart cracks and breaks within my chest. I sit down on the steps and lower my head into my hands and cry, mourning the loss of hope.

CHAPTER 27

The rest of the week, I'm merely going through the motions.

I finish up my next set of final exams. I go to work. I spend some time in the studio. But all the time in between, I spend staring at the TV like a zombie. I watch all my favorite Christmas specials, but none of them bring me any joy.

I spend a few nights at my parents' house, but I can tell they don't really know how to comfort me. They probably think I'm still messed up about Preston, but this has nothing to do with him.

When Saturday night finally comes, my mother surprises me with an extra hundred bucks to go to the salon and have my hair and makeup done for the dance.

"I know you'll want to look beautiful for Preston," she says, pulling me into a hug. "Show him what he's missing."

I smile and thank her, but it's not Preston I want to look beautiful for anymore.

As I sit in the chair going through this ritual of getting dressed up and perfect for a night out with Preston, I realize just how far I've come in the past couple weeks. How much Judd really changed everything for me in such a short time.

The fact that I used to worry about how I looked and what the label on my dress said so that I wouldn't feel like less of a person when I got into a limousine with people who were supposedly my friends suddenly strikes me as ridiculous. Having to put on a mask around someone automatically proved they weren't you true friend, didn't it?

I remember the way it felt to be around Judd's friends. How I didn't have to worry about anything other than just having fun and being myself.

That's what I want in life. That's the kind of friendship I want to find.

And the truth is that I don't know if it's more my fault or theirs. Did Preston expect me to act that way? Or did I only act that way because I was afraid he wouldn't like the real me? I put on a mask to try to fool him into believing I was good enough for him. But what if that mask is what ultimately drove us apart?

You can't truly love someone who won't even let you see their face.

"Oh, honey, you're ruining your mascara," the lady cries out. She dabs at my eyes and a couple of her co-workers come over to help fix the mess I've made of my face.

"I'm so sorry," I say. I blink and breathe in through my nose, pushing my sad thoughts out of my head so I don't make this worse than it already is.

"It's okay sweetheart," she says. "We'll get you fixed up in no-time so you can look perfect for your special man tonight."

I force a smile as the women wipe under my eyes and go to work replacing my makeup. But inside, all I can think about is that the one man I want to be with thought I looked perfect with tousled hair and no makeup in sight.

CHAPTER 28

I park in a guest spot outside Preston's apartment. I'm
running a little bit late and the limousine is already
stretched out at the edge of the curb, waiting.

I glance up toward Judd's window and for a brief
moment, consider making my way up there and letting
Preston fend for himself.

But then I remember the anger on Judd's face. How he
hasn't called me back or come by to see me to make things
right. If he really wanted me, he's the type of guy who would
have fought for me. I know it.

The fact that he hasn't so much as bothered to answer
the phone tells me all I need to know.

I walk up the steps to Preston's apartment, my body shiv-
ering in the cold. The sun hasn't even gone down yet and
already it's freezing. I hesitate at the doorway, making sure
my mask is firmly in place before I walk inside.

My group of friends is standing in the living room, drinks

in hand. They all turn as I walk through the door and I take a deep breath, then smile.

"Hi everyone, sorry I'm late," I say.

Preston crosses to me. "I'm glad you're here," he says. "The limo's waiting, so if everyone's ready, let's get going."

There's a flurry of activity as everyone downs their drinks, grabs their bags and coats and heads for the door. On the way down, Krystal loops her arm in mine.

"Bailey, we've missed you so much," she says. "What have you been up to? How come you haven't come out with us?"

I force a smile. I don't mention that I've been completely devastated and heart-broken for the past month and that I would have really appreciated one friend giving me a call or stopping by to see if I was doing okay.

Instead, I just say, "I've been working so much lately," I say. "And studying. My finals were ridiculous this year."

She rolls her eyes. "How hard can art finals really be?" she asks.

I grit my teeth, but keep my face calm. Normally, I would have laughed off her comment. I maybe would have thrown in some self-deprecating humor to top if off. Now, though, it just pisses me off. Doesn't she realize how that makes me feel?

"Well, you know I do take more than just art classes," I say. "Besides, I'd like to see you try to paint a self-portrait. Let's see how well you do."

Her hand slips out of my arm and she clears her throat. "Oh, well, gosh, I didn't mean anything by that," she says. "Of course you take more than just art classes."

Krystal and Summer look at each other, their eyes

widening and heads tilting to the side. I know that's silent speak for "What's gotten into her?"

"Your dress is gorgeous," Summer says once we're inside the limo. She holds her glass out while Preston pours champagne. "Where did you get that? I looked everywhere for that exact color of red."

"Thank you," I say, smoothing out my skirt. "I got it at June's. She pulled it off the floor for me so no one else would have it this year."

Summer's eyebrows go up at the mention of one of Atlanta's priciest boutiques. "I adore it," she says.

I can see the admiration glowing in her face.

Two months ago, I lived for these moments. I would have basked in her praise, feeling like I belonged here simply because I was wearing the right kind of dress.

Now, I feel empty. This moment is completely devoid of meaning because I know that there are more important things in life than dresses and impressing people who only put value in material possessions.

The fact that I realized this too late is what kills me.

I wish I had a second chance with Judd. I wish I could tell him that I'm ready to face my fears and be honest about my feelings if he would just give me the chance.

I stay quiet for most of dinner and by the time we finally get to the Wright's house and walk into the beautiful ballroom, I'm tired and wishing I could go home early. The room is so gorgeous, it takes my breath away and part of me is glad I didn't miss seeing it. The Wrights really outdid themselves this year. Instead of the normal, boring black and white ball, this year's crowd is full of colorful reds and greens and burgundies. The tree set up in the far corner is massive and beautifully decorated in gold and burgundy bows.

If I wasn't so sad and out of place, I'd be in awe of the beauty of this night.

Preston takes my hand and leads me toward his sister.

"Bailey, it's so good to see you," Penny says. She has a hand resting absently on her belly and I smile.

"You look so happy," I say. I hug her. "Congratulations on the baby."

"Thank you," she says. She radiates happiness and love. "I'm really glad you could come tonight. It's a really important night for Mason and I. Did Preston tell you about the charity?"

I shake my head. "What did your mom choose this year."

Penny shakes her head and touches my arm. "Would you believe she let me arrange everything this year?" she asks. "I got to choose the charity. Rachel's Kids is a new organization Mason and I started this Fall in honor of his sister."

"I didn't realize Mason had a sister," I say.

"It's a long story," Penny says. She lifts her gaze and waves.

I follow her eyes to the couple approaching us and my heart sinks deep into my stomach. I try to swallow, but there's a lump in my throat that won't let up.

Leigh Anne has her arm linked with a gorgeous guy in a tux. She looks as beautiful as ever with her wavy blond hair pulled up on the sides with crystal clips that shine in the light. I can hardly look at her without feeling guilty, and I'm really glad Preston is off talking to his dad instead of standing at my side right now.

"Hi Leigh Anne," I say, my smile tentative. I wish I could

somehow tell her I was sorry for her hurting her so long ago. I wish I could tell her that I'm trying to change, but this isn't the time or the place.

"Hi Bailey, have you met Knox?" she asks.

I hold my hand out to him and he shakes it. They look very happy together, which only makes me feel more alone than ever. I'm surrounded by people who have found their perfect match, and I've done nothing but ruin every single relationship I was ever lucky enough to be a part of.

The orchestra begins to play and couples drift toward the dance floor. I feel completely out of place despite having the perfect dress and makeup. I just don't belong here.

Preston finds me and pulls me onto the dance floor, and as he twirls me around, I wonder what I ever really wanted from him. Why did I think we were meant for each other? Why did I pretend for so long to be someone I'm not?

As we dance, I decide that after the music stops, I'm going to tell him I'm not feeling well and take a cab home. I can't do this anymore. I can't wear a mask anymore. From here on out, I just want to be myself. If some people can't appreciate and love me for that, then I'll seek out people who will.

But before the music has ended, Preston stops still at the edge of the dance floor.

I look up and see that he's staring at someone behind me. When I turn, Judd's hazel eyes meet mine and I inhale, my hands falling to my sides.

CHAPTER 29

"Judd," I say in a whisper. "What are you doing here?"

"You guys know each other?" Preston asks, looking between us.

I nod. "Yes. Wait, do you guys know each other?"

"Judd is the recipient of my family's research scholarship at FCU," he says. "Penny wanted to honor him and some of the other students who are working on a new treatment for leukemia since that's what Rachel's Kids is all about."

My eyes widen and I look to Judd. I can't find my voice. He was the last person I was expecting to see tonight. Why didn't he ever mention that his scholarship was coming from the Wright family?

"I'm sorry to cut in," Judd says, not taking his eyes from me. "But I need to tell you something. I've been trying so hard to deny it for the past week, but watching you here tonight, I know there's no use. I am in love with you, Bailey. And I don't care if Preston hears me say it. He may be the one you're with, but I can promise you that he will never love you the way I do."

I shake my head, not understanding or believing what he's saying. Am I dreaming?

"When you left me that morning, I thought maybe I rushed you. But when I heard you guys were back together, it destroyed me," he says. "I already lost someone to their ex once and I couldn't believe it was happening to me again. But watching you tonight, I know that this time is different. This time, I know I can't just sit back and watch you go back to someone who isn't right for you. I decided I had to put it all out on the line so that I'd never wonder what might have been if I had simply told you how I truly feel."

He starts to reach for me, but then pulls back.

I'm so surprised by what he's saying, I can't even set him straight about Preston. All I can do is stare at him, trying to understand it.

"Hitting you with the door that day was the luckiest, most wonderful thing that ever happened to me," Judd says. "Do you know how many days I sat there in the cafe trying to work up the nerve to talk to you? I daydreamed about you and talked about you so much, my friends were about to stage an intervention. I can't explain it, but when I looked at you, I knew you were mine. You didn't know it yet, but you belonged to me. With me. And then when you and Preston broke up, I wanted to ask you out so bad, but I saw how devastated you were. I knew I had to be patient. That you were going to need some time to get over him before you'd be ready to start something new. But that day we first talked in the science building, and then a few days later at the bar? I knew that I'd been right about you. About us. We belong together, Bailey. And I'll wait forever if that's what it takes for you to realize it."

My mouth hangs open and I struggle to breathe.

He'd been watching me in the cafe? He'd been coming there for me all this time?

Judd's eyes fill with tears and he turns away, his chest rising rapidly with each nervous breath.

I watch as he crosses the length of the ballroom and disappears into the hallway. I'm helpless to move or react, but there's a tugging in my core, telling me not to let him walk away thinking that I don't love him back.

I exhale and turn my head toward Preston, who is still standing there with his hand on my arm.

He raises an eyebrow and smiles. "What the fuck are you waiting for?" he asks. "Go after him."

My face breaks out in a smile and I lean forward and kiss Preston on the cheek.

Then, I kick off my shoes and run.

CHAPTER 30

I find him outside on the porch.

He's leaning against one of the large white columns and I rush toward him, stopping just short of the edge to catch my breath. I have no idea what I'm going to say, but I hope I'm not too late.

"Judd," I say, breathless.

He turns and slowly, a smile pulls at the corners of his lips.

Hope flows through my heart like a spring. "Don't go," I say.

He cocks his head to the side. "I'm not going anywhere," he says. "I'd wait for you forever if that's what it took."

I shake my head and step toward him, my feet cold against the wooden floor of the porch. "I'm not dating Preston," I say. "We never got back together."

His eyebrows twitch and his hands open and close at his sides. "You didn't?"

"No," I say, biting my lip. "He asked me to come to this

dance a really long time ago. He came into the cafe to remind me of our plans. It was the same day I had made such a fool of myself by practically running out of your apartment. I was going to tell you about the dance, but you never answered any of my calls."

He takes a step toward me. "I was working on this project," he says. "I'm working with a group of research students and they called me into the lab just a little while after you left my apartment that morning. I don't have cell service in there and by the time I left, it was too late to call. The next morning when I got to the lab, Penny was there talking to someone about the upcoming dance and finalizing the plans for tonight. That's when I overheard her saying something about how you and Preston had gotten back together and were coming to the dance."

"We never got back together, I swear," I say.

"But I saw you on campus together. He kissed your forehead," he says. "It looked like—"

I shake my head. "He kissed my forehead because I was crying," I say. "He thought I was crying for him, but I wasn't. I was crying because I was so scared I'd lost you. That I'd messed it all up by running away. I'm so sorry about that. I've just never opened myself up to someone that way. I've never been so real around anyone in my life. The things I was feeling for you were stronger than anything I'd ever known and I wasn't sure what to do with that. I was so scared that if I went any farther or if I really gave myself to you, I'd never be able to survive the pain of losing you."

He reaches for me, pulling me into his strong embrace. Our breath mingles in the freezing air and our lips meet.

Warmth surges through my body and I wrap my arms around him, clinging to him.

"I was so scared I'd lost you," I say.

He cups my face in his hands. "Never," he says. "I can't explain it, but I know with all that I am that this is fate. We were meant to be."

"I love you," I say. "I never believed it could happen this fast, but standing here, I know it with all of my heart. I love you, Judd Kohler."

"I love you, too," he says.

He pulls me closer and as we kiss, I vow never to hold anything back from him again. To embrace the fear of getting hurt. To face it head-on.

I remove the mask I wore for so long and stand before him, flaws and all, knowing that I've finally found someone who will love me just the way I am.

EPILOGUE

Judd sits behind me as I work.

My shirt is splattered with paint and my hands are caked in red. It's Christmas Eve and I'm painting a scene from the Christmas Memories Charity Ball for Penny to auction off.

"Are you always this messy when you create?" he asks.

"Shhh," I say. "Don't judge my process. You'll scare off my muse."

He laughs, then clamps a hand over his mouth.

"And yes, I like to use my hands in some instances instead of always using brushes. Art can be messy. Deal with it."

His phone rings and he steps into the hallway.

"Sounds like fun. Let me ask her," he says when he comes back into the room. "Do you want to go to Brian's? Everyone's hanging out, playing games and stuff."

I smile and wipe paint on my jeans.

"Are you challenging me to a dance-off?" I ask.

A corner of his mouth lifts in a sexy, challenging smile. "Maybe."

I smile back. "Challenge accepted."

He laughs and tells his friends we'll be there in a few minutes.

I wash my brushes and put away the paints, then grab my coat.

"Did you want to go home and change?" Judd asks as we make our way through the quad toward the parking lot.

A sense of freedom washes over me and I shake my head.

"No," I say, looking down at my loose, paint-stained clothing. "I'm all good."

He smiles and pulls me closer.

We make it halfway across the grass before it begins to snow.

ABOUT THE AUTHOR

Sarra Cannon is the author of several series featuring young adult and college-aged characters, including the bestselling Shadow Demons Saga. Her novels often stem from her own experiences growing up in the small town of Hawkinsville, Georgia, where she learned that being popular always comes at a price and relationships are rarely as simple as they seem.

Sarra owns her own publishing company and has sold three-quarters of a million copies of her books. She currently lives in Charleston, South Carolina with her programmer husband, her adorable redheaded son, and her beautiful daughter.

Love Sarra's books? Join Sarra's Mailing List to be notified of new releases and giveaways!

Also, please come hang out with me in my Facebook Fan Group: Sarra Cannon's Coven. We have a lot of fun in there, and I often share exclusive short stories and teasers in the group.

Want more? Come join us LIVE several times a week on my YouTube channel.

Connect With Sarra Online:
www.sarracannon.com